RANGER

ROADBLOCK!

Stone slowed the bike. Five men stood in front of him with rifles, old and coated with dirt, in their hands. Stone edged his finger toward the trigger of his front-mounted .50-caliber machine gun.

"Just slow down there," one of the men screamed. "Tell us where you're heading and what you're carrying in the back of that there contraption."

"Sorry, fellas," Stone said, his eyes fixed on every one of them, "I'm coming through. Get those roadblocks out of my way or I'm taking them out."

"Please be my guest." The man laughed and swept his arm toward Martin in a mock bow.

Stone tilted the bike in a flash and pulled his finger hard on the trigger. The .50-caliber spat out a mouthful of slugs that tore into the wooden planks and sent them rocketing into the air. He pulled out the Uzi 9mm from his left shoulder holster and slammed in the clip and started the bike forward.

Most of the crowd froze, but the leader and his main man leveled their rifles at him. Stone ducked beneath the low bulletproof visor on the front of his bike and with his right hand let loose a two-second burst of fire...

Also by Craig Sargent

The Last Ranger #2

Forthcoming from
POPULAR LIBRARY

THE LAST RANGER

CRAIG SARGENT

POPULAR LIBRARY

An Imprint of Warner Books, Inc.

A Warner Communications Company

CHAPTER ONE

A body lying in a ditch.

The body of a man, or what had once been a man, although now it was hard to tell just what he was, so covered in blood, so battered and torn the flesh. Around the body lay other bodies equally indistinct, as if somehow all the features that they had once possessed, all the wrinkles and lines and expressions they had exhibited in life, had been wiped clean from them as chalk is wiped from a blackboard, leaving not a trace of what has been. They were just things now, no longer human, as they waited with infinite patience to rot down into the hard, cold ground beneath them.

Around them scurried countless vermin, rats and roaches, spiders and centipedes, digging out their due with fangs and pincers from the bloated flesh. The smaller scavengers raced in and out of the nasal passages, eyeless sockets, and wide-opened mouths of the dead, bringing their bloody pieces of

torn carcass out on unsteady legs, greedily carrying loads even larger than themselves. The rats, the mice, the lizards feasted on the outer flesh, stripping off layer after layer of the dark brown skin, rotted to the loose, dripping consistency of overcooked pumpkin. Straight lines of ants marched two hundred feet into the shadowy woods, where they deposited their cargo of putrid flesh and then headed swiftly back for more. In the shimmering heat clouds of the noonday sun, the corpses almost seemed to move their half-consumed hands and faces as the jaws of the scavengers jerked out chunks from deep within the recesses of the foul-smelling cadavers. It was as if they were puppeteers pulling the strings of the corpses' muscles and nerves, acting out a grisly show for none to see.

Yet though the vermin slowly disassembled the corpses piece by bloody piece, they left the one in the ditch alone. Occasionally, a cat-sized rat would approach and sniff the body with blood-coated whiskers, its black nose vibrating rapidly, seeking the scent of decay . . . but then it would leave. The lizards, the ants, the bloodworms sent out their scouts, but these also returned, seeing that this one was not quite ready to be taken, sensing that by the sheer purpleness of the bruises on the body, by the flow that continued to trickle like melting red snow from a hundred gashes and rips in the skin that this one still lived—barely.

A centipede, thick and bloated from its feast of blood but tired of the battle over what remained of the corpses, rowed itself forward on a hundred scampering legs toward the ditch and the motionless body that awaited it there, a feast untouched. It stopped by the bloodied head and looked at it for a moment, not quite sure where to start. Then, dimly re-

membering in its dust-particle-sized brain that the pink things of the last corpse had tasted good, it reached out with razor-sharp pincers and snapped shut around a good-sized piece of the prone body's lower lip.

"Jesus," the recipient of the kiss croaked through lips as dry and cracked as a salt flat as the pain shot through its nerves, bringing it out of the blackness somewhere between coma and death.

"Get the fuck off me," the voice spat out, somehow lifting its right hand, coated with an oily sheen of blood, and slamming it down on its own lip. The palm made contact with something squirming and wet, and the vile blood drinker released its grip on the flesh as the hand swept it away into the air. It landed five feet off in the dirt and quickly paddled back to the other bodies, where the food didn't fight back.

The body lay groaning softly for several minutes, scarcely daring to allow itself to come into full consciousness as the pain it felt in every part of its torn flesh was too intense to bear. No part of it had been left untouched, no swatch of flesh unpainted by its own blood. But there is nowhere to hide within one's own self, and so the nearly dead man at last opened his eyes just a crack and almost screamed as the slashing rays of the sun bit into the blood-filled eyes that had been closed for hours.

"God, God," the body intoned over and over as memory flooded into it like a tidal wave of debris. It didn't want to know, didn't want to think back to those last few hours, those minutes when all was lost. Martin Stone didn't want to remember that his entire family was dead—and he was the reason why.

He tried to rise, but fell back down like a sack of cold

bricks. Nothing worked. His arms, his legs felt like rubbery things which he could only make jerk around without any real strength. He was used to being strong. To be like this— like a fish out of water, easy prey for anything that stumbled along—it was too horrible, too terrible to contemplate. Why wasn't he dead? Why hadn't he succumbed to his wounds like the others?

"God, you bastard, I'm ready to die! Take me! Take me now!" He screamed out the words with all the energy his dehydrated throat could muster, but only a whisper emerged, barely audible even to himself. Whether God was dead, or just not interested in this particular brand of human misery, who could say. But nothing happened. Only the slurping and tearing sounds of the foul beasts working on the nearby bodies answered him—and the smell of burning rubber and plastic from the still-smoldering Winnebago twenty yards off.

He tried not to think of what they were eating—but he knew. His mind filled with images of their torn flesh, their faces eaten away down to the bone. His stomach and chest racked spasmodically and he cried—rather, he *tried* to cry. But no tears dropped from the bruised and swollen eyes, for there was not a drop of moisture left within him for such luxurious functions.

He tried to shut off the valve of his emotions and waited to fall back down into the black pit from which he had just emerged. But the sheer pain of his body kept him awake, stabbing him in a hundred places, torturing him against his will back into full consciousness. And each moment the memories, the faces of those he loved loomed larger in his mind, filling him with a fury that he could not express.

They had been in the Winnebago, he and his mother and

sister, heading toward Denver when the motorcycle gang had struck. The slime had appeared out of nowhere, a wolf pack of black-jacketed psychos out for fun and blood. Chills ran down Stone's spine the moment he spotted them, for they hardly looked human—more like something one would dream on a bad, bad night. Their faces were scarred with the battle wounds of countless fights. Broken bottles had sliced up chins and ears, fists had smashed noses into twisted, hanging stumps, jagged scars ran the length of necks and jaws as if they had been sliced in two and sewn back together again. And on the backs of each of their chain-covered jackets, in garish Day-Glo colors, a grinning purple skull floated over a red mushroom cloud. Below the cloud in the same blood-red were the words GUARDIANS OF HELL.

The gang roared toward the Winnebago and surrounded it, screaming at the top of their lungs as they waved pistols and machetes in circles over their heads, their faces flushed with excitement, their half-toothless mouths nearly salivating in anticipation of the fun they were about to have. Martin floored the unwieldy vehicle as dishes and books flew wildly around in the back cabin, crashing loudly. Reaching under the dashboard, he whipped up the 12-gauge sawed-off Browning that sat there and blasted out the window at the closest riders. He managed to get two of them, knocking the bastards right off their cycles, sending their bodies flying sideways in a bloody spiral.

But then they were on him. They jumped from their bikes onto the speeding Winnebago, grabbing its doors and side. Suddenly one of them appeared at his window and reached inside with a long curved hook, trying to snag him. The meat hook dug deep into Martin's shoulder, and when the pock-

faced biker ripped it back, Martin's entire body was slammed sideways into the door, ripping his hands from the wheel. The Winnebago came to a lurching stop in a weed-covered field just off the road.

After that it was just a blur—a terrible mesh of screams and pounding blows as they kicked and pummeled him around the ground like some sort of football. He could hear the cries of his mother and sister as the pigs took their fill. Then a booted foot descended on his head, darkness filling his eyes until there was nothing else. He had blacked out, sure in his last second of consciousness that he had seen his last of this life.

Why wasn't he dead? He had fucked up ... fucked up bad—and now they were gone and he wasn't. He mentally cursed himself again, sending waves of hate deep into his body, trying to make himself die through sheer effort of will. His father had been right all along. For years he had fought the dominating personality of Major Clayton R. Stone as the two of them had matched will against will until at times they almost seemed enemies rather than father and son. And all the time that Martin had been so sure that he himself was right, he had in fact been wrong. Wrong about everything. The old man had seen it all as clearly as if he had been looking in a bloody crystal ball. And now it was all too late. The moving finger writes, and having writ moves on. And not all your tears nor all your protestations shall change a single word of it.

He breathed out a sigh of infinite disgust at all the damage he had caused, all the mistakes he had made, and let himself sink down into the cold dirt, giving up his feeble attempts to rise. He would just lie here and wait for the creatures to finish

with the others. Then it would be his turn. He let his mind go blank, not even feeling the intense pain any longer. He would be gone soon——and he deserved to die. The sooner the better, good riddance, and all that rot. But the words of his father echoed through his brain like bullets ricocheting back and forth, no matter how hard he tried not to listen.

"Don't go out into that radioactive wasteland, Martin. It's filled with nothing but murderers, madmen, flesh-eaters— and worse. Stay here in the bunker until the savages have killed each other. Then the world will be yours and your sister's for the taking. But for now you must—stay—here! Here you will all be safe. Here, here, only here!" The stern face of his father seemed to turn into a flock of blackbirds which flew wildly about Martin, scratching with the claws and fangs of memory. His mind filled suddenly with countless images, impressions of his life shooting through him like a film reel that had jumped its sprockets and was projecting random images at super speed. Good—he was dying. They said your entire life flashed before you as your soul left its bed of flesh. He went with it as the years spun by in a storm of near madness . . . went with his memories as he waited to die.

CHAPTER
TWO

He was two. He was lying in his down featherbed in their sprawling family mansion not far from Denver. He was holding his stuffed hound dog tightly against his chest as he heard his mother and father screaming at one another in the other room. His father was hollering that he had to go—it was his duty. And his mother was yelling back that he had already given enough, that he should give to them—to her, to their son, Martin. Tears welled up in the boy's eyes that his daddy was leaving again to go to some far-off magical land called Vit-nam, wherever that was. Dimly, he wondered if he had done something wrong to make his father angry at him and that was why he was going. In his young mind he searched for the wrongdoing. Was it the dishes he had broken days before? Was it because he had pulled the tablecloth and they all fell with such a thunderous roar? Was that why his father was leaving?

He was now three. It was Christmas and the snow was everywhere and the world was bright with rainbow streams of light. The streets were bustling and filled with laughing people, all buying their last-minute presents. Martin felt as if he would burst with joy. All was right with the world. His father and he were walking down the streets of Denver and Martin felt proud. Proud because his dad stood so tall above him like a human skyscraper, and in his Special Forces uniform and beret he looked just like a real soldier on TV. His father showed him the different store windows filled with dancing reindeer, with Santas flying down from the heavens, sleighs filled with toys. He lifted Martin high in the air and the boy squealed with delight as the world spun around him like a top.

Suddenly nasty men were around them. Men with cruel faces and hard words. They rose from their motorcycles parked along the curb and said things to his father. Things Martin didn't understand but knew instinctively were meant to hurt.

"Hey, soldier boy. Just back from Nam? Kill many gooks recently?"

"Thinks he's tough-shit macho, right? Hup—two—three—four, hup—two—three—four."

"Hey, ain't that a Special Forces hat? You man enough to wear it?"

Martin's eyes widened in fear, but his father ignored them. Holding the boy cradled in his arms, he started forward. The memory was fuzzy after that. Three of the men, almost as big as his father, stood in their way and reached for Martin, laughing, their mottled, stubby faces looming toward him like the bogeymen of his nightmares. Without even putting Martin down, his father lashed out with several quick strikes

to their faces and throats. Three bikers fell to the street. From that day on, Martin Stone was in awe of his father. And perhaps, deep inside, not a little afraid of him as well.

Major Clayton R. Stone, Ranger, Special Forces, war hero, and multimillionaire, was a complex and contradictory man even to those who knew him closest, even to his son, Martin. Capable of the most lavish bursts of generosity, he could also spend weeks or months brooding, almost incapable of human warmth or interaction. Perhaps it was his own childhood that had forged such a multisided character, a personality that ran the gamut from hot to cold on a daily basis so that neither those around him nor perhaps he himself ever quite knew just what he was going to be like on any given day.

Clayton Stone had known he was different from the other kids almost from the day he was born. It wasn't just that he was the son of a millionaire and heir to the Stone Munitions Company, nor that even as a child he was big and powerful, with tremendous strength and intellect. There was a purpose to him, a direction that seemed more fitting to a man than a mere child, an unquenchable thirst for knowledge of everything around him. Even in play with the other kids, in the mock battles that boys seem to universally engage in, it was always Clayton who was the leader, the one giving orders, leading charges up sandy slopes, and it was Clayton who would stand victorious on the top of the conquered hill, gazing down around him as if in a trance. It was as if he was always trying to see just a little beyond the here and now, beyond what the other boys saw, as if he were training himself for some future destiny that he alone knew.

Perhaps it was part of Clayton's volatile and stubborn

nature to resist all that his own father had planned for him—
going to Harvard, the gradual shifting of the family business
to him. But it wasn't for him—none of it. And when World
War II broke out, with the radio announcement of Pearl Har-
bor, Clayton, age fifteen, packed a single suitcase of clothes,
left the family mansion in the dead of night, and headed off
to enlist. When the Army sergeant arrived at the recruiting
office in Denver at eight-thirty in the morning, he found
Clayton, using an expensive leather suitcase as a pillow, asleep
in the doorway. Clayton was nearly six feet two inches tall
before he had reached his sixteenth birthday, so the sergeant
didn't bother to ask the lad for his birth certificate. And
Clayton signed on for the biggest conflagration in human
history. By evening he was on a bus to boot camp.

If ever a man had been made for the military, it was Clayton
R. Stone. He took to basic training like a duck to water, never
complaining, looking forward to the firing practices, the long
marches, the wet tents and freezing rains that the other men
abhorred. His gung-ho attitude was contagious, and he quickly
caught the eye of some of the officers on the base—particularly one Major Bamberger who was doing some recruiting
on his own. It had already been recognized that this was
going to be a special war with special needs. The days when
lines of regular troops wearing brightly colored uniforms fired
away at each other as bugles blew in the background was
gone. Gone forever. Swallowed up in Hitler's blitzkriegs.

"Son," Bamberger had said to Clayton one month after he
had arrived in boot camp, "you've got the makings of a fine,
fine soldier. Now, I've got just one question to ask you. I'm
here to recruit men for what is going to be the toughest bunch
of bastards in this man's army—the U.S. Rangers. It's going

to be bloody, dangerous work. And your chances of coming out alive are a hundred to one—no, make that a thousand to one. But I can promise you one thing—you'll get your chance to fight, and you'll make a difference."

"I want to see action, that's all," Clayton answered without hesitation. "I just don't want to end up sitting behind some goddamned desk 'cause my IQ is too high for me to be used in combat. If you can promise me that, then I'm ready to go anywhere on this planet."

"You want action?" Bamberger had laughed loudly, slapping the young soldier on the back. "My friend, get ready for a roller-coaster ride into hell."

Corporal Clayton R. Stone was in England in two days, in a secret training camp twenty miles inland from Liverpool. Under the tutelage of Major Lowery of Her Majesty's Special Services, he and his all-American regiment were put through a training course that made U.S. boot camp look like a Girl Scout overnight. It included everything from rock-climbing exercises and rappeling to knife and hand-to-hand combat, canoeing, parachuting, survival techniques, surveillance, espionage, and booby traps. But more than anything, they were taught to be tough inside and out—and to kill without a moment's hesitation, for the enemy they faced was ruthless, without even the trappings of humanity. They would have to be worse.

After six weeks of sixteen-hour-a-day training, they were taken thirty miles out into the English countryside and tossed out of their trucks with only knives and compasses and the shirts on their backs. Stone was the first one back in camp.

The next few years could only be described as a tornado of blood, in the center of which Clayton R. Stone found

himself flying. As a Ranger he saw action throughout Europe. He was dropped behind enemy lines countless times, parachuting down in the dead of night to carry out recon and sabotage. The Nazis almost got him a dozen times—but somehow they didn't. While men died all around him, Stone grew tougher and meaner, spending months with small five- and six-man units of Rangers as they wreaked their havoc throughout the Axis-held continent. When D-Day came, Stone and his compatriots were dropped behind the German defenses along the Normandy beachheads, where Clayton took out thirty Germans and three pillboxes singlehandedly, opening up a whole section of cleared beachhead for the invading Allied forces.

While Patton sped north through France, Stone was already in Germany helping prepare the way by cutting Nazi communications lines and blowing bridges and railroad tracks to cut off the enemy's possible retreat. He was one of the first in Berlin, moving building to building in a desperate search to find Hitler before the Russians. And then it was over. The most destructive war the world had ever known had ended. The most destructive weapon the world had ever produced had ended it. Lieutenant Stone looked around him and realized there was no more fighting and that in the five years of war he had turned from a naive teenager into a man. He also realized that he hadn't the foggiest idea what he wanted to do with his life.

But a brief stint in his father's munitions company (which had grown tremendously during the war), attending its meetings and acting like it was all supremely important—whether or not the profit margin was accelerating with the inflation rate—bored him to tears. Though Clayton was one of the

most important men in Colorado and was courted by scores of beautiful women, it all made him sick. Slowly, he realized with a curious mixture of horror and excitement that he loved war. He had never felt more alive than when he had been out in the backwoods of Europe fighting the Nazi vermin, and like many returning soldiers he couldn't get out of his mind the memory of being so electrically alive, of every sense working on overdrive, of pitting himself in the ultimate test of life and death.

After six months of trying to adjust to being a rich civilian, Clayton R. Stone reenlisted, much to the shock of his father and family. But the moment he touched foot on an Army base, smelled the cordite from the firing ranges, he knew he had done the right thing. For better or worse, it was in his genes to be a soldier, a killer of other men. And no one was better at it than him.

But in the years following World War II, the fighting man was not needed as the United States channeled all its energies into building the American dream that its boys had died for. Televisions, cars, a house, a dog, and 2.3 children per family— these were the new goals as all America marched full speed into the War of Acquisition. And Clayton R. Stone found himself reading papers on "The Role of the Commando in War" at ill-attended, overlit auditoriums in the Pentagon. But he stayed on, for he knew that man was not the civilized creature that the optimistic fifties was trying to paint him out to be. He knew there was a Cold War blowing its frosty breath across the landscape and that it would someday turn hot. He knew that soon, for better or worse, men like him would be needed again.

When the Korean War broke out, Stone demanded to be

sent to the front immediately. Though it seemed initially that they were going to kick the communists all the way back to the Yangtze, the situation quickly degenerated into a bloody stalemate in which the bodies of thousands of his fellow soldiers were fed like beef into a grinding machine. Before he knew it, they were coming home from a war that Eisenhower had decided was unwinnable and to which he negotiated a costly settlement. But a new scent of blood, of might trying to smash right, was brewing in a hitherto virtually unknown little hellhole of a place called Vietnam.

Stone was one of those over there from the first—training the Vietnamese Army to do *meaningful* reconnaissance, to fight the VC at their own game—out in the field. But as the war progressed and more and more American troops joined in the fray, he took over training of a new generation of American fighters, first in Special Forces, then in the LRRP units—Long Range Reconnaissance Patrol—which he was instrumental in helping to form and define. For, from his experiences in World War II, Stone believed firmly in the need for small units of highly trained men capable of going off on their own for weeks, even months at a time, into the jungles, into North Vietnam itself. As far as he was concerned, the only way to defeat Charlie was to play his game better than him.

Unwilling to ask those under him to do anything he wouldn't do himself, Stone went out with them, taking the riskiest, the most suicidal missions, much to the displeasure of his superiors. But by then his years of working with the Vietnamese, his knowledge of the politics of the war had given him an understanding of just how to get things done, one way or another. He and his six-man team traveled fast and

light, carrying only super-stripped-down weapons and virtually no supplies. For the way that Stone fought was the way of living off the land, of sleeping in grass beds, of eating the local food, be it bamboo shoots or beetles. Those who could stomach it he kept. The rest were sent back to their base camps for reassignment—without dishonor. For he, above all men, knew that only one out of a thousand could make it out there.

While the rest of the regular U.S. Army forces were stomping around tearing the country apart but not inflicting any mortal wounds on the enemy, and while the politicians wrestled with the antiwar movement back in the States, Major Clayton R. Stone was deep in the jungles of North Vietnam and Cambodia, against U.S. law, making quite a name for himself among the North Vietnamese and their Vietcong cadres. Wherever he struck, he left only fire and bodies and the heads of his victims atop stakes. Stone knew that this war was not just a war of bullets and cannon, but a war of psychology, of fucking up the other side's head—just as he was trying to fuck up yours. And the Major blazed a trail through Asia that scared the black pajamas off half of the communist brigades convoying supplies and men up and down the Ho Chi Minh trail. He was called "The Head Taker—*Dinh Trau*," though none had seen his face, and all prayed to their communist god that they never would. For none who had seen him was in any condition to describe the death-dealing American.

But even Stone was human, though some of his team might have challenged the notion. In March of 1970 he walked directly onto a well-concealed punji trap and drove three of the feces-coated bamboo stakes straight up through his foot.

His men carried him nearly twenty miles on their backs, taking turns as they grew tired, and called in a med chopper. Within hours he was in Da Nang, his wounds cleaned, with antibiotics pouring into him by the quart. It was close. Vietnam was a country that seemed to just be waiting for a cut, a wound on every American there so it could send in its legions of rot and fungus and infection. Stone fell into a deep coma, his fever rising as high as 106 degrees. The surgeons called in the chaplain.

But the man who had wiped out countless enemies of his country was not about to let himself be taken by a few microscopic VC. His life force fought back with the strength of a tiger as his body poured out sweat as if he were in a steam bath. By the fourth day the fever had broken. If the VC wanted him dead, they'd have to do it themselves, not with a bamboo proxy.

Perhaps it was because he was in a weakened state when he awoke, or perhaps the painkillers they had given him had gone to his head, but when Stone opened his eyes, he swore he was dead. For standing above him, with the deepest blue eyes and the reddest hair he had ever seen, was an angel.

"I knew I'd make it up here," Clayton managed to whisper. "This is heaven, correct?"

"Try Da Nang Hospital," the nurse coolly replied. "About the farthest thing from heaven on this earth." But Stone had been struck, for the first time in his life, by pure, unadulterated love. And being the kind of man he was, he pursued Jennifer Donohue with an intensity and a sureness of purpose that was unstoppable. They were married three weeks later. A month after that she was pregnant and Clayton insisted she

head back to the States. Although feeling something of a deserter, she did so. The next year Martin Stone was born.

The situation in Vietnam was getting worse all the time. Clayton still did his thing out in the bush, but it was obvious to him that the public sentiment back in the U.S. and the fact that the ARVN couldn't get their act together to oppose the North meant that the country was lost, that all the blood, all the human sacrifice made by his fellow countrymen had been in vain. Increasingly bitter, he carried out his assassinations, his sabotage with a vengeance, as if he just wanted to see how many he could kill before the war was over. And before he knew it, first the Army was pulled out and then in spring '75, the rest of the advisers, the special units like himself.

He blew his last bridge in the North and headed south with his six-man team, knowing the ball game was over. They shot down the coast in a commandeered North Vietnamese troop transport, just miles ahead of the invading communist army, and Stone knew they had to reach Saigon before the Reds did or they were dead men. On the road they passed about thirty captured Americans being marched down the road, hands on their heads, an advance unit of the North Vietnamese Army smiling happily behind them. Stone looked around at his team, and to a man they nodded assent. It was a bloody, costly battle as the six-man team was outnumbered by nearly fifty North Vietnamese regulars. But when it was over, twenty-five would-be prisoners of war found themselves on a truck heading home instead of in some godforsaken hut with bamboo slivers being forced under their fingernails.

They made it to Saigon literally by the skin of their teeth, escaping in one of the last choppers. It made Stone sick to

his stomach to see the Vietnamese who had fought alongside them for years clinging to the skids of the choppers, to see them falling from the sky screaming, as if it were raining men.

CHAPTER THREE

Clayton Stone was given the Congressional Medal of Honor in a Washington ceremony, along with five other men. The President himself stood there and shook hands with each of them. Jennifer stood in the front row, holding little Martin in her arms as she watched the event proudly. Even though the rest of America might not welcome the boys home as heroes, she did. For she knew, having served over there, what it was really like, and the hell that America's best had gone through.

But Major Stone found nothing to feel good about in all of it. The politicians, the generals had messed up a winnable war until it was a cesspool of corruption and inept leadership. Then they had deserted an entire nation, leaving thousands of the men and women they were pledged to protect to horrible deaths. But the worst of it was that there were still American POWs over there. And no one seemed to give a flying fuck.

"Sir, I feel I must speak up," Clayton said when President Ford came to him and placed the medal around his neck. The President's aide looked at Clayton with great distaste, pursing his lips as if he had just sucked a lemon.

"Really, not now, Major," the man said. "Protocol forbids—"

"Screw protocol," Stone said with barely repressed fury. "I'm sorry to be so rude, but there are still men, prisoners of war, over there. I *know* there are—don't you understand?" He spoke with desperation, pleading, wanting the President to hear, to feel his concerns. "I know because I saw them myself."

"Yes, yes—ah—Major Clayton," Ford had stuttered as he looked at the nameplate on Stone's jacket. "We're doing all we can." With that, he gave Clayton a wickedly dumb smile and moved on.

Stone quit working for the armed services of the United States the next day. As a soldier he couldn't speak freely, but as a civilian he could. He went to work putting all his energies and tens of thousands of dollars from his personal trust fund, which was worth over a million dollars, to help the poor bastards who'd been left behind, relegated to the garbage heap of history. He'd make America listen—whether it wanted to or not. He sent out letters, appeared on radio shows, gave speeches at American Legions. But it was all to no avail. The country was getting over the first war it had ever lost as well as its first resignation of a President. The entire nation was in a state of shock. It was passé to even talk about POWs or MIAs. This was the Me generation. Take care of yourself and let God take care of the others.

But Stone kept on, obsessed with those who had been left

behind. For nearly two years he continued to send out press releases, to make all the waves he could. Exactly twenty-two months after he returned from Vietnam, the threats began. At first they were innocuous enough—phone calls telling him to calm down and forget this whole MIA-POW stuff.

"Times are changing," the unidentified voice on the phone said. "We can't keep having all these old war wounds opened up. It just creates hysteria. You understand, Major—hysteria."

"Fuck off, asshole," was Clayton Stone's crude but to-the-point reply. But the calls continued—and grew increasingly antagonistic. Gradually, it dawned on Stone just who it was— the CIA. Their plan for the eighties just didn't include bringing up the past. This was a new breed of fool, Clayton realized, men who were more interested in function than honor, more interested in trade deficits and double-dealing alliances than the lives of their own front-line soldiers.

Major Stone came home one day and found his wife in tears. It took him nearly an hour of gentle coaxing to get it out of her, but he finally did. She had received two calls threatening her and Martin with unknown but clearly unpleasant consequences unless Clayton ceased his efforts.

The Major went to his room and took out his .44 from a locked drawer. He stayed up the entire night debating whether to go after the bastards. He knew he could find them if he had to and blow their fucking heads off with a blast that would be heard around the world. But he also knew how it would read on the front pages of the papers, how it would play on TV—just another Viet vet who had cracked. And his family, his son would live under a banner of shame for the rest of their lives. When the dawn sun broke, he glared

out at it as if it were an enemy. He looked haggard and, in his own way, terrified. He had always been able to carry out that which he knew was right. For the first time, he couldn't.

After being heckled and hit with several rotten vegetables and fruits at a Veterans Day speech he gave two weeks later about the need to honor America's fighting dead and to do anything, even risk another war, to get back her imprisoned sons, Clayton had had enough. Screw them all. The realization that all the men he had seen die had already been forgotten, that their ultimate sacrifices on the battlefield weren't worth two cents back in the money-sucking land of America, pushed him to the brink of madness. His entire life, the personal philosophy on which he had based everything— freedom, truth, loyalty, all of it was apparently obsolete, for suckers and fools and cracked vets who held pistols in their hands and stared at the moon with a rage that colored the sky red.

He stayed indoors at their sprawling mansion and brooded. Jennifer grew increasingly worried about the man who had always been such a dynamo of energy and life. Now he moped about, sitting in a dark corner of his study, chair facing the wall and a map of the world—just sat, saying nothing, sometimes not coming out for an entire day. It was as if he were going over his entire life, searching for something. She knew he felt confused, hurt by the reception his country had given him, had given all of them. He had been out of touch over there for nearly a decade. Things had changed.

After weeks of his own personal hell, Stone managed to battle the demons within him into submission. He emerged at last from his mahogany-paneled cave with a grim but determined expression on his craggy face.

"If this is how they want to play the game—then so be it," he told his wife. "But don't let this nation ever come to me again for help because I'll spit in its goddamned face." He put his medal, his gun away, put all the accumulation of his years in his country's service into boxes, sealed them, and pushed them far back in the attic into shadows where they could not be seen. All that he kept was the beret with both the Special Forces insignia and his own Rangers flash on the side. This he wore from then on wherever he went, as if daring any man to try to knock it off.

Having made some sort of peace with himself, Clayton Stone joined his family's munitions business and took over the helm, much to the delight of his aging father, who had already had two strokes. With Clayton running the show, the company doubled its profits every year, branching out into sales overseas, into the development of the most modern and technologically advanced weapons systems for infantry, armor, and air. To those in the know, the name Major Clayton R. Stone, retired, represented one of the foremost weapons producers in the world. To the man in the street, he was an eccentric, barrel-chested elderly fellow with his green beret tipped at a cocky angle and a chip on his shoulder.

But at least it all gave him more time to be with Martin— and April, the baby girl his wife gave birth to. One afternoon he looked up and realized that he hardly knew the boy. And Martin was suddenly shooting up like a spring root, seeming to grow inches every time his father turned his head. Clayton began spending time with his son in the backyard playing ball, jogging with the youth. The Major had always been skeptical of fatherhood—but now that he was a father, he

found the role allowed a softer side of him, a side that had been hidden beneath the warrior, to come out.

But love also brought fear—fear that the boy was being raised into a world that was heading for the grave in a bobsled. The fools who ruled seemed to know less and less what they were doing at the same time they built more and more nuclear bombs. Clayton knew one thing without a shadow of a doubt—as bloody and dreadful as the wars he had fought in had been, there would never be another like them. The next war would not be fought between men. It would not be fought at all. One day there would be civilization—the next day there would not. A man wouldn't have to die to visit hell.

Without consciously realizing it—at first anyway—Clayton began trying to train the boy, then just reaching his teens, to perhaps be able to exist in that brave new world. He began teaching him, very slowly, the things that he had learned through a life of fighting and killing. They started with simple sparring. Martin came home with a bloody nose one day, saying that the school jerk, three years older and a foot taller, had slammed him against the wall and punched him. His father spent that entire afternoon, and the next and the next, showing him basic boxing and sparring techniques. By the fourth day, when Martin passed by the brawler and the boy reached out to grab him, Martin decked him with a single right hand. The fat kid fell on his ass and stared up as if he had just been enlightened in a very unpleasant way. He never bothered a Stone again.

Clayton was proud when Martin walked in that afternoon with bruised knuckles. He had been in enough scraps to know the signs. But the boy seemed almost ashamed of the incident.

"I didn't enjoy the feeling of my fist hitting his chin,"

Martin told him when his father asked him to describe the fight blow for blow. "I'm sorry, Dad, but I don't think I want to learn any more of your tricks. I know it's hard—I mean me being the son of a war hero and all that—but in all honesty I don't want to fight anymore." With that the training was abruptly ended.

To Clayton it seemed as if the entire world around him had joined in a conspiracy of cowardice, of dim-witted pacifism, of thinking that if one just ignored the dark side of human nature, it would go away. He retreated even more into himself, never really understanding that it is the universal nature of children to oppose their parents, to be different from them, whoever and whatever they are.

For Martin, this meant that all things to do with the military, with war, with being tough and a good fighter, were things he fled from. Instead, as he hit puberty and shot up into a strong, handsome teenager almost overnight, he spent his time in the school swimming pool, where he became captain of the team, and with girls, of whom there always seemed to be a ready supply. The last thing he wanted to do was worry about the next world war. Having never known war, the need to prepare for it seemed absurd. And like ninety-nine percent of the planet, he believed that if the nukes rolled in, not all the training or survival tricks in the world were going to help one iota.

CHAPTER FOUR

Major Clayton R. Stone appeared the same on the outside, but on the inside he became a hardened, bitter man, feeling, rightly or wrongly, betrayed by his generals, his country, and his own offspring. He could see now he had become obsolete—a joke—with his beret, his stiff military bearing, his tendency to bark out orders at company meetings of Stone Munitions instead of showing the smooth, ass-kissing demeanor that the top VPs and administrators who worked around him did. He was too intelligent not to see it all, and inside he bottled up the pain of being an anachronism, bottled it up like a fine wine that he would someday pour when the time was right.

But though the hedonists, the yuppies, the buy-now-pay-laters of America all tried to do their best to pretend that life was just one big game of upward mobility, an endless succession of nights on the town, the Cold War between the U.S.

and the U.S.S.R. grew frostier and frostier until the air was filled with the smoking breath of two dragons on a collision course.

With the breakdown of the last remaining SALT treaties and the Russians' increasing paranoia about the "Star Wars" Defense System initiated by President Reagan, the Reds undertook to arm themselves at an ever-increasing rate until they were producing fifty new atomic weapons a day so as to be sure to get through any high-tech shield the Americans could throw up around themselves. Naturally, the United States had to respond once again in kind. By 1988 nearly seventy-five percent of each nation's gross national product was being siphoned off into high-tech weaponry and exotic research as each tried to find a power that lay beyond nuclear—as if they needed something more destructive. What they both sought was the antimatter bomb.

In March 1988 the European Military Coalition and the Third World Alliance, comprising between them seventy-four nations from around the world, issued a joint statement condemning the accelerating increase of the nuclear arms race. They vowed to intercede in a military capacity should either America or the Soviets attempt a nuclear attack on each other or anyone else. The entire planet hovered on the brink of oblivion as the prayer, "Now I lay me down to sleep, I pray the Lord my soul to keep. If I should die before I wake, I pray the Lord my soul to take," took on a certain ironic significance, for hundreds of millions of human beings did lay their heads on their pillows each night wondering whether they would in fact see another sunrise or just the burning fires of the man-made sun come to consume them in its atomic teeth.

On the sly, Stone came to a decision that he would try to survive the inevitable war. And he would make his family do so too, whether they wanted to or not. He began the design and construction of an immense fallout shelter in the foothills of the Rockies at the northern end of Estes National Park, one of the wilder sections of the Rocky Mountain range. Though only 150 miles northwest of Denver, the land, fifty acres of it that had been in his family's possession for decades, was never used and rarely visited. It was so hard to reach that the trucks bringing in loads of alloy metals, plumbing, electrical materials, insulation, and a thousand other things could only get within fifteen miles of the place. Then all their materials had to be laboriously loaded by hand onto Land-Rovers and jeeps and hauled through the woods and up and down slopes for hours before the site was reached.

Not that any of the men on the work crews complained. They were being paid double for the extra effort, the aching muscles, the mosquito bites, the occasional rattlesnake sinking its poison-filled fangs right through somebody's boots. But Stone was going to build something that would work, whatever the cost, not some dinky little showpiece that would grace the cover of one of the country's many survivalist magazines. Those would all be blown away like bubbles when the breath of the atomic giants roared out death on the final night of civilization.

It took a year, but when it was completed the Major was proud—and sure that whatever the experts said, he and his would survive. It was buried between two mountains, each towering a good half mile on either side, and had been sunk right into the base of one of the granite slopes using dynamite and pneumatic mining drills. With natural rock walls four

feet thick on the one exposed side and containing its own underground spring, the thing would be able to withstand anything but a direct hit. The shelter was basically four rectangles forming one large square, with a total space of 19,789 square feet. Each rectangle would be used for a different function—one for living space; one for machinery, i.e., electric generator, air- and water-purification systems, radio, geigers; an open space for plants and exercise, including a circular jogging track and weight room; and a storage room filled with weapons, light and heavy—everything from handguns to long-range rifles, automatic weapons, heavy machine guns, antitank equipment, and whatever the hell else Stone decided would be a nice toy to take into the next stage in the evolution of mankind. In this last space crates of ammunition were piled from floor to ceiling. Clayton had seen truth in its rawest form—on the battlefield. There had always been one rule by which mankind lived and would continue to live until the end of its existence—those with the biggest guns lived; the rest died—or became their slaves.

By the end of 1989, it was clear that war was just around the corner. You could smell it in the air like the unbreathable dankness before a thunderstorm. The Major once managed to drag his entire family up to the complex, and though they seemed impressed with the effort that had been put into it, they were hardly thrilled with its aesthetics or its function. Stone tried to get them all used to the idea that they might soon have to go to the shelter, bringing the topic up at dinner or just out of the blue. They went along with it, letting the old man make his little speeches as they passed the bread or changed the channel. They all half believed he was going batty, getting a bit senile, perhaps from being hit in the head

too many times out there in the wilds. Stone could see that they were just humoring him, but it didn't matter. For as the rest of the world went on with its trivial pursuits, its mundane anxieties, Clayton Stone's thoughts were already in the post-nuke world as he tried to plan for every eventuality they would face.

On the morning of February 13, 1990, Major Stone woke from a nightmare and bolted upright on the thick goose-down mattress in the master bedroom of the family mansion. It was time!

"Wake up, wake up, Jenny," Stone yelled, shaking his wife, who groaned tiredly on the bed beside him.

"What, honey? What," she asked, her eyes still closed, hoping he wouldn't make this one of his full-fledged anxiety attacks so she could go back to sleep, back to the sweet dream of flowers and an afternoon picnic when she was a little girl back in her home on the banks of the Ohio. It would be the last sweet dream she would ever know.

"It's—it's time to go," Stone said, rising and ripping off his pajamas as he walked across the room. "We have to leave tonight, all of us, immediately. I know it's coming. I can feel it in my bones. Get dressed, there's no time to argue," he screamed, reaching over and ripping the comforter from her body.

"Jesus fucking Christ," Jennifer yelled, her body instantly covered with goosepimples from the cold air seeping in beneath the window. Outside, the north wind beat out a frantic rhythm against the side of the house, whipping the skeletal branches of the trees around like tapping fingers on the windowpanes. Jennifer realized suddenly that she felt odd herself. Very odd. As if the pit of her stomach were falling

out, as if she were on an elevator that had just slipped from its anchorage and was plunging down.

Stone opened his drawer and took out the .44 magnum in its holster, holding it for nearly twenty seconds as he stared at it in sudden horror. Although he had planned for it all, had believed it was going to happen, now that it was it all seemed too awful to imagine. The entire world gone. Everything they loved and cherished, every memory, every babbling brook, every sight and smell every human on earth had ever known would all be gone into a common funeral pyre of atomic flames.

"So be it," he said almost in prayer and strapped the gun around his waist. He grabbed the five eight-round clips from the drawer and pushed them in one of the pockets of the down parka he had thrown on. Then the beret. Just the flicker of a bad smile crossed his face. It was going to be like old times.

"Take your thirty-eight," he said to his wife, who was glaring at him as she sat half dressed on the edge of the bed. "We have one hour to pack and get out of here. We'll take all three vehicles. You can drive the RX-7, I'll take the Mercedes, and Martin and April can handle the Winnebago. Got it?"

"Yeah, I got it, I got it," his wife muttered as she suddenly speeded up, realizing she had only one hour to pack everything that mattered to her in this world. Major Stone shot down to the second floor, banging on doors, stamping on the floor as he went. They'd all be pissed as hell, but waking them like this would get their adrenaline going and would put their senses on full alert. And they'd need everything they had—of that he had no doubt.

"Martin, we're going. It's time, son. Get up, get your stuff. Everyone can bring four suitcases."

"Going where, Dad?" Martin asked, dreading the answer, dreading the possibility that his father had finally cracked.

"You know the hell where," Stone said gruffly. "This is no time for playing games, son. Minutes could mean life or death."

"I'm not going," Martin said, sitting up in the bed and crossing his arms across his broad chest. "I've got too many things to do tomorrow. There's a swimming meet. You know I'm the captain. I can't go running off on one of your wild-goose chases. I mean really, Dad, how do you know what—"

"Martin," Stone said with such quiet intensity that his son stopped talking in midsentence. "I've never ordered you to do anything in your life. I've never hit you, unless we were sparring. But I'm telling you now—we're in an emergency situation whether you believe it or not, and I am taking the God-given power that a father has and I'm ordering you to come with me now." He stood just feet from the bed, looking down at Martin with an expression that his son had never seen before—and didn't like.

"I'll tell you what, sir," Martin said, exploding his lips on the word "sir" so as to mock it. "I'll come with you just to keep peace in the family—just so my mother and sister won't have to see one of us get hurt. But when we get there and when the missiles don't come—which they won't—I'm leaving. Leaving for good. You understand? I never want to talk to you or see you again."

"Fine. If that's what it takes for you to come, so be it. I think you misunderstand me, though, Martin. I've never

wanted war to come. I would give my own life to stop those fucking H-bombs from coming—to save you and April and Jenny and this whole stinking world. But they are coming and I can't stop them. We will live, like it or not—all of us here in this house will live."

They were on the road within an hour and twenty minutes, the three family cars loaded to the rafters. They hit the interstate and headed north through the cold night the 150 miles to the shelter. Stone knew the others were ready to forget that he was their father—but it didn't matter. None of it mattered, as they would soon find out, God help them all. Stone's premonitory dream felt stronger and stronger in his mind. He had been too close to death not to sense the chill of its proximity.

They reached their exit from the highway just as the sun hobbled up over the horizon on cloudy crutches. Then they turned onto the back road that took them another ten miles until they came to the piece of muddy track that was their road. They had to go slowly along the bumpy, winding passage that weaved its way over hills and through granite canyons, taking them sometimes thousands of feet up with a sheer drop down as far as the eye could see only feet from their dust-spinning tires. It was hard going, but Stone had wanted it that way. He knew what humanity would turn into after the war. The more hidden they were, the safer, both from the bomb and from the radioactive living dead who were left.

Stone turned on his car radio as they passed Pointer's Peak to the right, stretching up above them with its snow-tipped granite cap. There was a lot of white noise at first from the shielding effect of the iron-ore-rich mountains of the Rocky

range, but at last he narrowed in on a static-filled voice that sounded as if it were coming from a million miles off. And the man sounded hysterical.

"This is no joke—Jesus God I wish it were," the DJ said, and Stone could sense the tears falling from the man's eyes as he spoke. "I repeat, we have received word from around the nation that missiles were seen shooting up from numerous silos—and heading toward the Soviet Union. The government has thus far refused to comment on—"

"Damn!" Stone yelled, slamming his fist down on the dashboard so hard that he cracked the bone, creating a hairline fracture that shot a bolt of pain through him. But he didn't even take notice of it, so great was his rage at the fools who had run the world. All they had to do was not get us into an atomic war. Let them lie, steal, do all the things that politicians had been doing for the last five thousand years. But the only thing that mattered they had fucked up.

"Wait, wait," the DJ said breathlessly, hardly able to speak. "I've just received word that a launch has been verified. I repeat, ladies and gentlemen out there—it's over. The United States and the Russians have launched an all-out attack on one another. I—I—" The man seemed to collapse totally into tears for a few seconds before he regained his composure. "I'm sorry, I'm sorry, I've never had to announce a nuclear war before. I'm afraid I don't quite know how. What's that? Oh—I've been advised to tell you that you should switch to one of the designated Emergency Broadcast stations. So I guess . . . that's a wrap. Well, I probably won't be speaking to you anymore . . . so thanks for listening and remember who loves ya. Uncle Alfie—loves—you." With that the DJ broke

into a gush of tears and the station disappeared from the air, swallowed up instantly by the static.

Fool, Stone thought. Why doesn't he get his family, head for the hills. At least try—do *something*. He felt no sympathy for the man. His tears were a masochistic luxury. To all those who would sob their last seconds away or reach for the booze or the drugs so they could see the end in a happy blur, let them die. Only those who fought to live would survive. Darwin's law of the jungle had just become the only law left.

Clayton Stone knew they had only half an hour at most before the first incoming nukes hit. They should be all right even outdoors, with the Rockies creating a virtual mile-high wall around them. Still, if one came too close or went off in the atmosphere nearby . . . He pushed the Mercedes faster, making the others increase their speed as the three vehicles shot around rock-strewn trails that only a mountain goat could feel secure on. Stone hoped none of the others had turned their radios on. It was better that they be angry at him. The reality of war, of the end of all they knew could crack any of them, make them incapable of functioning.

Suddenly there were no more secrets. The dawn sky, filled with big cottony slow-moving clouds painted orange and pink, burst into fire. It was as if the clouds themselves had caught fire as they swirled wildly, writhing around like things alive, things in pain. Within a second they grew blindingly bright, their moisture evaporating out in glowing steam escaping in every direction like volcanoes in the sky. Within another second the clouds were gone and a pure whiteness took their place—a whiteness so intense and profound that one felt as if the burning fires of hell had suddenly risen up from beneath the ground and taken over the heavens. Stone instinctively

shielded his eyes, praying that the others were doing the same. At the same time he counted under his breath, "One alligator, two alligator," so as to gauge the distance.

The super brilliance above faded to a throbbing orange, and Stone started the car forward again, the others, he could see through the rear-view mirror, following. The entrance to the shelter was just ahead when he heard the first roaring thunder roll in. "Two hundred and fifty alligator," he finished. So the nuke had gone off about fifty, sixty miles off—Fort Collins, the Air Force base there. Men, jet fighters—all just super-accelerated atoms now spinning off into the galaxy.

He pulled the black Mercedes to a full stop about thirty feet from what looked like a sheer rock wall and took a small transmitter from his jacket. He aimed it at the rock face and pushed a button. The radio signal instantly caused the four-foot-thick granite wall to split into two walls which rolled apart without a sound until there was an opening ten feet high and wide. Stone started forward, motioning through the car window for the others to drive in behind him. Their journey was over. And when the last of them was inside, Clayton pushed the transmitter button again and the mountain wall closed behind them.

CHAPTER FIVE

The women cried for days. They just sat on couches in the living room in front of the fake fireplace with glowing logs—the real heat was created by solar power alternating with gas heat, all regulated by computer—and sobbed their eyes out. Martin didn't say a word to anyone and only glared at his father whenever he passed by. But Stone knew it was all necessary. He had seen countless men lose their best friends, their brothers. Now they had lost the whole world. The body, the human soul had to mourn or it would go mad. So the Major left them all alone and tended to the functioning of their new home.

After five days he gathered them all together and told them what the future held in store.

"For better or worse, we're going to live. Nukes have struck all over the country, so your friends, our town, every-

41

thing is gone. I'm not telling you this to depress you even more, but just to prepare you for what is to come."

"I don't know if I want to live anymore," April said, her body curled into a ball on one of the couches as if she were trying to just disappear.

"Me either," Martin spat out with disgust. He was still in mourning for his girl, Rita. The thought of her sweet body dissolved into burning atoms was something he just couldn't digest. "I think it might have been better for all of us if we'd died along with everyone else out there."

"Look," Stone said very slowly, "I'm not saying things are great. In fact, they're horrible. I fought all my wars to save us all from this. Obviously, it didn't do too much good. But they're dead out there—and we're alive. We have supplies and fresh-water systems to last years. It's going to be depressing, maddening. We're all going to hate one another at times, but we have to go on. We have a responsibility not just to ourselves to survive, but to the human race itself. We may be some of the last human beings with unmutated chromosomes. The very existence of humanity may depend on us."

"I don't give a damn about humanity," April cried out, jumping up from the couch. "They deserve to die. We all deserve to die." With that she ran from the loft-sized living room off to her bedroom, from which she didn't reemerge for two days.

But none of them did kill themselves. The human instinct for survival is the strongest of all programs that nature outfits us with. Otherwise Homo sapiens would have become extinct long ago. Somehow the Stones adapted to life in their mountain home. Clayton Stone had equipped it not just with food

and medicine but with comforts, luxuries that he knew the others would need to retain their sanity—tape decks and large color TV sets with a full catalogue of movies and audio cassettes, a library filled with over ten thousand books—the classics, along with various technical manuals on every subject on earth that, for all Stone knew, could end up being one of the last repositories of human knowledge. He had also installed hot tubs, a steam room, and an immense futuristic kitchen containing completely computerized equipment with which Jennifer soon became immersed as she tried to develop recipes that could make basic food staples taste wondrously different. Her instincts to be the archetypal mother, the nurturer, were taking over, pushing her dark desire to die deep within her soul.

Only Martin continued to hold a fierce grudge against his father, as if blaming him for all that had happened. After a month of waiting for the teenager to come out of it, Stone at last took him aside, into the gymnasium that none except the Major had taken advantage of thus far.

"What's the problem?" he asked.

"What's the problem?" Martin answered with that thick sarcasm that seemed to drip from every word he spoke now. "The problem is that I live on a dead planet, and I happen to be alive. The problem is I have a super-macho father who thinks he's so fucking tough that death is going to be scared off. I got news for you, Dad. We're already dead. Only, we just don't know it."

"And you think it's my fault?" Stone asked calmly.

"You and those like you who thought that war was ever going to create anything but more war. Yeah, maybe I do

43

blame you," Martin said with a grim snicker. "Maybe I just do."

"Like to take a poke at me?" Stone asked. "Maybe it is my fault."

"Dad, I know you were tough as nails once. But that was years ago. I think I might hurt you now."

"Then come on," Stone said, standing up from his wooden chair so he was facing his son, who was nearly as tall as him but not quite so broad. "Punch me for all those poor people who died out there. Punch me right in the face for having destroyed everything you love."

"I don't think so," Martin said, suddenly backing off a little with a sheepish expression on his face. But Stone could see he had struck a nerve.

"Hit me for having killed Rita. She's dead, Martin. Dead as a slab of cold rock." Stone didn't want to torture his son, but he knew that if Martin didn't release the pent-up anger inside him he would freak out, hurt himself or those around him.

"Goddamn you," Martin screamed out and charged his father, his fists ripping toward the deeply lined face. But the Major hadn't fought for a third of a century without learning something. He easily blocked the punches and slid to the side, pushing out with his arms so that Martin fell to the astro-turfed floor of the gym.

"Come on, son, punch my goddamned face in. Avenge all those melted masses." The teenager leaped from the ground with the speed of a leopard, but though he was fast, he was completely unfocused, charging in with abandon. Stone caught one of the wild roundhouse blows in his right hand and swung his hips around so they slammed into Martin's stomach. With

a quick, smooth motion he flipped him forward so the youth landed on his back on the cushioned floor several yards away.

"Goddamn you, god-fucking-damn you," Martin screamed out in frustration as he charged again with all the fury, all the pain he had kept bottled up inside of him exploding out, goaded on by his father. But though the strength was there, the ability wasn't. Again Major Stone blocked and this time swept him down to the ground with a quick kick. He dropped down on top of his son, pinning him with a knee to the chest and his arm in an elbow lock.

"I'll kill you, I'll kill you," Martin screamed out, his eyes filled with waves of tears. He flailed about within the narrow confines of his father's hold in a state of near hysteria as all his grief poured out in a single, uncontrollable burst.

"You want to kill me—okay," Stone said in a whisper. "I'll teach you how. I'll teach you everything I know until you're better than I am. And then if you still want to, you can come and get my goddamned ass."

The weeks turned into months as time lost all meaning for the four members of the Stone family. The women went on somehow, occupying themselves with cooking and mending things. April, after moping for six weeks, at last took out the art supplies her father had brought to the shelter and went at it with a vengeance, painting scenes of the world—the world she remembered and wanted only to remember—filled with meadows and flowers and rabbits and deer staring out with wide, dewy eyes. Clayton and his son, Martin, went at it like Marines in boot camp. Using his son's anger as the fuel to make him work, the Major began teaching him everything, from the fighting arts to the use of all the weapons that were stored in the munitions sector of the shelter. The youth, at

the start anyway, wanted only to kick his father's ass and put all his energy, his total concentration into what his father showed him. For hours each day they went at it, sparring, working at cleaning pistols and automatic weapons, and making their own bullets and explosives.

More than anything else, Stone tried to ingrain in his son what he himself had learned—how to survive, how to kill the other guy. How to live off roots and leaves, how to make medicine from herbs, how to find water, direction, warmth. How to make fires by using a cartridge, how to set traps for game and for men. How to scout, surround, and carry out an attack on an enemy—even one of vastly larger numbers. Major Stone showed his son that there was a way, a method, to accomplish anything.

Life somehow settled down, in its own bizarre fashion, to a routine.

April and Martin spent five hours a day at studies, as if they were still going to school. Jennifer, who had been a schoolteacher for several years in her younger days, guided the two of them, creating programs of study, giving them tests and essays to write. It was a life, a life not worthy of too much close scrutiny—but for now it would have to do.

Months turned to years as life slowed to a crawl. At first the rest of the family would ask Clayton almost weekly what the radiation levels were like outside, or if he'd picked up anything on his shortwave radio. But they always got the same answer: the world was highly radioactive right outside their mountain home, and no, there was nothing on the radio except static. There was no one out there. They would have to stay ten, even twenty years inside, then perhaps once the rad levels had dropped to even a possibility of sustaining

human life, they would emerge again to see what was left. After six months they all stopped asking.

The training went on and on, every scrap of information, of fighting and survival knowledge passed from father to son until at last Martin knew, as he filled out into a strong man, that he could beat his father. But he didn't demonstrate it. The Major, now in his late sixties, prided himself too much on his strength, his speed, for Martin to dissuade him of the illusion that gave him the will to live. He still looked relatively young, acted the same, and tried to instill in his family that same burning will to survive, to persevere, that filled his veins like burning lava.

But all men are mortal. When the end came, it came in a flash. They were seated together at dinner, canned ham au gratin and vegetables from their supply of canned produce sitting on the table in steaming platters. Major Stone said grace as he always did, ending with, "God, grant us the ability to stay human and not revert to savagery—and the will to do so."

They were the last words he ever spoke, for his eyes suddenly grew wide and he slapped at his chest in a clear motion of pain. As they reached toward him, Major Clayton R. Stone jumped up in his chair as if he were about to run off, and then just as suddenly he fell forward, slamming into the table and pulling the tablecloth and dishes with him as he tumbled to the floor. Martin was beside him, giving him mouth-to-mouth, slamming the heel of his hand onto the broad chest. But it was all over. He knew, just by touching his father's flesh, that he was gone. The grand soldier was dead. He had gone into that other world from which no man had ever returned.

After the grief and the tears and a burial in a rear section of the shelter, the three of them went back to the living quarters, sat in front of the fire, and looked at each other with questioning expressions.

"What now?" Martin asked the question out loud. Neither his mother nor sister could answer as they sat dumbstruck. Their father had been such a guiding force, a sun around which they revolved, that now that they were on their own they hadn't the foggiest idea what to do.

"Well, I have something to tell you both that I don't think you're going to like," Martin said, looking down at the rug. "After Dad's funeral, I checked the radiation meters—something the Major always did—and they were normal, totally, completely normal. And the records of the readings for each day going back three years are all normal. Much of what Clayton told us was clearly false. There are people out there, I'm sure of it. Lots of them. The man was mad, trying to keep us trapped in here forever, his own personal guinea pigs. We'll die if we stay here. I will—or go mad. I'm leaving tomorrow. If you want to join me, you're welcome."

They elected to come with him. Somehow Major Clayton had always managed to take their attention away from the reality of their situation. Always talking, being optimistic, getting them going in projects. Always doing something so they wouldn't have time to think. But now that he was gone, the whole place seemed suffocating, like a coffin. They hardly felt able to breathe.

The next morning they loaded into the Winnebago, one of four vehicles that were parked in the bunker garage, and headed outside for the first time in five years, two weeks, and three days. Martin pushed the radio controls and the stone

walls slid apart. They all squinted as they drove outside, used to artificial light, not the brilliant ball that hung in the sky like a floodlamp. But within minutes their eyes had adjusted, and they smiled and laughed aloud as they saw the woods of the Rockies all around them filled with growth and wildlife.

"How is it possible?" his mother asked Martin. "The radiation readings were so high."

"It was all fabricated, Mom," Martin answered. "Or to use another word, it was a lie. I don't know exactly what Father had in mind, but I think he wanted us to stay in there forever. Maybe his mind snapped."

"Don't say things like that about him. I forbid it," Jennifer said harshly. "He gave everything he had for us, and I'm sure he had some good reasons for all that he did."

"Well, think what you want," her son answered just as harshly. "But the Geiger attached to the front of the Winnebago is showing almost zero rads."

"Where do you think we should go?" April asked, seated between her mother and Martin on the wide leather seat.

"Denver," he answered without hesitation. "For Christ's sake, maybe everything is the same. Our house, the town, the high school. Rita," he added softly. "Maybe all this hiding out has been for nothing."

"Just because there's life out here," his mother said a little nervously, "doesn't mean that it's friendly. Could be bandits, cannibals, God knows what."

"Relax, Mother," Martin said with a self-assured scowl. "If there's one thing Father did, it was teach me how to fight and kill and maim. I've got a shotgun right under the dashboard here. We'll be okay. I promise you, there's nothing to worry about."

CHAPTER SIX

Blood began flowing from Martin's mouth again as he lay on the cold dirt. Yeah—everything would be okay, he thought, grimacing as the stabbing pains in his chest and neck brought him back from his reveries. So, okay that they were all dead, being consumed by beasts just yards away. I might as well have killed them myself, taken out my own gun and shot them, he accused himself, remembering again the warnings his father had tried to instill in him over the last five years. But he hadn't listened. It had all been like water dripping from his ears.

Sometimes something will occur to a man, and in a second his entire life will change. The very way he perceives reality, his own history will be unalterably affected. His life, Martin realized, had been a power struggle against his father. Not just battles against learning all the tough-guy stuff, but battles against the very nature of the way his father had perceived

the universe. For Martin had wanted to believe that everything was okay, that basically people were good and that the future would work itself out. He had been wrong.

He heard the sound of heavy animal breathing and somehow twisted his neck to the side to see a silver-haired wolf gazing down at him, its breath steaming out in the frosty morning air. Its eyes burned like red stars, staring at him with the magnetic attraction that all predators feel for their prey. It started forward, loping cautiously toward him until its jaws were just above him. Though he had just prayed to die, now that death was actually staring him in the face, Martin had second thoughts. He yelled out with all his might and threw his hand up to scare the two-hundred-pound bundle of teeth and silver fur off. It worked—but just for a second, as the startled creature jumped back several feet. But it was a hunter. Martin's gesture had revealed to it that he was hurt, could not fight back. That was all it needed to know. The wolf closed in for the kill.

He turned instinctively away from the long canine teeth coming at him and covered his face with both hands. Just let it happen quick, please, God, quick. Then the musky body was on top of him. He gritted his teeth, his stomach muscles tightening in anticipation of the fangs sinking in. But nothing happened. He waited a few more seconds and then gingerly opened his eyes. The thing was dead, lying atop him like a rug that needed spraying for fleas. And dead center through its skull, going in one ear and out the other, was an arrow with luminescent red and blue feathers sticking out the end.

"What the—" Martin gasped as two figures wrapped in thick furs came forward and leaned down toward him. They

were Indians. "I, I . . ." he stuttered, having not the faintest idea in the world what to say.

"Quiet," one of them whispered. "No talk." With that the man reached down and grabbed hold of Martin's jacket and with a single heave hefted him up over his shoulder. And Martin Stone, every cell in his body in agony, fainted into a merciful darkness where there was no sensation.

He had no idea how long he had been under as he seemed to slide up and down a pole with light at the top and utter blackness at the bottom. He knew if he fell it would all be over, so he climbed and climbed with every ounce of his being, and the light grew closer until at last he broke through it like something hatching from an egg. His eyes slowly opened, and looking down at him from above were a pair of the biggest brown eyes he had ever seen on the face of one of the most beautiful women he had ever laid eyes on.

"Shh," she said, putting her fingers to his lips. "Do not talk. You are very weak. You were near death many times. But now you will live." She smiled, and Martin couldn't help but be entranced by the bronze Indian face with its delicate features, large, sensuous mouth, and black hair which cascaded down and over her firm, ample breasts pressing out from within her buckskin jacket.

"How long have—have I been under?" he asked, feeling his lips crack as he spoke.

"A week," she answered, holding his head up and feeding him water from a gourd. "They all said you were as good as dead, but I put herbal salve on your wounds and got my brother to perform his magic on you."

"Magic?" Martin asked with a grunt.

"Yes, he is the tribe's medicine man—very powerful. To him you owe your life, for he worked over you for nearly three days, using all the healing ceremonies of the wolf."

"Yes, I remember some face swirling around me, a mask with horns. I thought I was dreaming. Who the hell are you people?" Stone asked as he rose up on his elbows and looked around. He was inside some sort of tent made of animal skin, lying on an odd assortment of furs with a small fire glowing in the center of the twenty-foot-wide structure.

"We're the Muache, a tribe of the Utes," the woman replied, sitting up on the crude lashed-branch bed Martin was lying on. "We've been in Colorado for nearly a thousand years, until the white man blew half of it up. Now we no longer have anything to do with the world outside. Let them all kill one another. We live here on what was called our reservation. Now it is our land. And we defend it with guns. We live our own life. White men do not dare try to take what is ours."

"But your people helped me," Stone said as he tested his various joints and appendages, surprised to find that everything was still in working order, albeit stiff as unoiled gears.

"You were lying wounded, about to be eaten by the wild beasts. Our code of honor demands that we help any man threatened by the beasts. It is not the way for a man to die. Had you been walking and well, the braves who found you would have killed you."

At the word "kill," Stone's mind suddenly flashed back to the memory of the massacre of his mother and sister. "Oh, God," he groaned, slumping back down onto the mattress and covering his face with his hands. "Better that they had

left me for dead. As soon as I'm able, I'm going to put a bullet between my eyes."

"Don't dare talk like that," the Ute woman yelled, reaching forward and slapping him across the face with a crack of her hand. "The gods have granted you your life a second time. It is not for you to question them. A man must carry out his fate—not run from it. Do not act like a frightened child and make me ashamed that we saved you."

"You don't understand," Stone said softly, unable to meet her eyes. He told her what had happened. "You see, I might as well have executed them," he said when he'd finished. He tried to rise and walk but fell down on the floor. She helped him up.

"That's right, Superman," she cracked. "Try to walk with one fractured leg, a smashed elbow, a hundred assorted wounds, and a bruise the size of an apple right next to your spinal cord."

"And how the hell do you know so much about human anatomy?" he shot back angrily.

"I studied to be a nurse," she replied, "before the war—before I came to the land to be with my people. We have returned to the old ways here. Perhaps in a terrible way it was good for my people that the war happened. Before, the people on this reservation were on welfare, many of them were alcoholics. It was not unusual to see them sitting in front of the concrete hovels built by the federal government, just staring off into space. Now they are a proud hunting people, living with the land, as they did for centuries. In your infinite stupidity, your people did us all a favor—took us out of the gutters of our souls and restored us to our proper places in the universe."

"Stop saying 'your people,'" Stone suddenly yelled out. "I didn't press the fucking buttons. For Christ's sake, I marched in a few peace demonstrations. My whole family is gone. I lie here broken into little pieces, and now you want to blame me for the crimes of those who have already paid with their own lives."

"You're right," the Ute woman replied. "It's just as prejudiced of me to blame you for the war and the breakdown of so-called American civilization as it was for whites of the prewar days to accuse my people of being genetically shiftless and lazy. Who can say what really lies in a man's heart until he is given the opportunity to prove himself. But now, white man"—this time she said the words with a friendly mocking tone—"you must sleep."

"I'm sorry," Stone said, suddenly feeling ashamed for his generally antagonistic attitude. "You've been wonderful to me, and I'm acting like an ungrateful clod—a stereotypical Caucasian." He smiled slightly. "What's your name?"

"I'm Chama." She smiled back at him.

"Chama," he half whispered, growing tired. "It's a beautiful name. I'm Stone—Martin Stone."

"Hello, Mr. Stone," Chama said with twinkling, startlingly alive eyes filled with the liquid sensuality of an animal. She handed him another, smaller gourd and made him drink from it and then tenderly placed his head back down on the fox-fur pillow. He tried to protest, to rise again, though just what he wanted to do, or where he wanted to go, he had no idea. But the moment his head touched the soft, strangely sweet fur his eyes snapped shut and he dropped once again headfirst into darkness.

When he awoke, the flap of the tepee was open and the

sun was streaming through. There was no one in the tent, so Martin rose, stepping naked from beneath the pile of furs. He walked around a few steps, testing his legs, his body. Though parts of him still ached, everything worked. He searched around and found his clothes, freshly cleaned and folded, and put them on.

He stepped from the tepee into the sunny world with a cold expression on his face. He couldn't get the death of his family out of his mind. It seemed to fill him like a disease. He walked forward, stumbling shakily on legs unused for nearly a week. He felt as if he had been reborn—risen from the dead, from the old world into the new.

There were about fifty tepees spread out around a wide clearing at the edge of one of the dense Rocky Mountain forests. They sat in groups of three, forming semicircles along the curving treeline. The sandy open space in the center of the village of buffalo-hide tents was filled with Utes carrying out their myriad duties. Women hauled loads of firewood from the forest, while those with children sat stitching clothing or making repairs on the tepee hides that had gotten a little moth-eaten here and there. They sat around the many fires constantly kept burning over which fresh-killed hides were dried, food was cooked, and babies kept warm as older children ran back and forth playing bow-and-arrow games with unstrung branches, their half-naked bodies glistening with sweat.

It was like a scene out of a Currier and Ives print from a century ago, and it hardly seemed possible in the late twentieth century. And yet . . . He walked among them, attempting a feeble smile but was met with a wall of silence and scornful eyes. They didn't seem to like him much. He was probably

the first white man who had been allowed on their land since
the last bumbling bureaucrat had stumbled by before the war.
They had saved him, but they obviously didn't want to be
friends. With a sheepish expression he sat down in front of
one of the fires to warm himself and get some of the winter
sun, as his skin felt pasty and dead from the many days
indoors.

Even the children pulled away from him as if he were a
leper, and for the first time in his life, Martin Stone, having
grown up in wealth and privilege, felt what it was like to be
an outcast, an unwanted member of society. But he could
hardly blame them. Their ancestors had lived a millennium
in harmony with the land and the animals they hunted. The
Caucasian race had managed to fuck things up completely in
just a few hundred years.

Suddenly he felt that he had to prove something—prove
that not all whites were capable only of destruction. It was
as if he were the elected representative of his race. And
whether any of them would give a good goddamn, he didn't
even care. Stone rose from the warm seat by the fire and
headed off to the woods. Within minutes he was carrying
back an armload of dry firewood that covered his chest and
face. The Utes pretended not to watch, but he sensed them
keeping the evil eye on him as he half stumbled up to one
of the main woodpiles in the tribe's central square and dropped
his load down. Without a moment's hesitation, he headed
back again.

He spent the entire afternoon carrying wood, ignoring the
eyes, the glances of the dark-faced race of unfriendly strangers
around him. He moved tons of the plentiful fuel, breaking
off branches, snapping them into yard-long pieces, and load-

ing up. His body ached, but it felt good. He could feel the blood, the oxygen surging through him from his efforts, healing him, bringing back life to every part of his wounded flesh. And somehow the work cleansed him, cleansed his mind of the burden of guilt he had been carrying like the bodies of the dead themselves on his shoulders.

As the sun fell from the purple sky in a muddy red ball, the Ute braves came out of the woods with the rewards of their hunting expeditions—coons, rabbits, foxes, three stags, and an immense bison which five braves pulled whole on some sort of primitive dolly. Stone realized that everything they used was of primitive design and building material. Surely they had guns, traps from the old days. Yet they carried only bows, spears, and long hunting knives at their sides. He ignored them as they passed by with their game, and they ignored him with frozen, statuelike faces. Yet, still Martin continued his two-hundred-yard trek back and forth down the long hill filled with daisies and weeds to the woods below and back again. He didn't even know why he did it now, so exhausted were his muscles, so tired and unthinking his brain cells. But at least the labor stopped their faces from spinning around him and kept the ghosts of his mother and sister at bay.

As he moved past the fires, the leathery-faced squaws looked at one another and clicked their tongues like a flock of cackling hens. Surely the white man was as mad as a prairie dog that has eaten loco weed. But deep within their eyes was a grudging respect for the fool, for he seemed to have the strength, the single-minded focus of the Indian.

By evening he hardly knew where he was as his legs trembled and weaved like stalks of wheat from the strain of

the 150-pound loads he kept carting. He had made a pile next to the central fire a good twenty by twenty feet wide and nearly ten feet high—enough to feed even these ravenous flames for months. The Indians sat around the warmth of the sparking tongues of yellow and red that reached up into the darkening skies as they ate their dinners. They watched the white man with amusement, the braves back from their hunts, smirking at the man who did woman's work.

After his fiftieth, or sixtieth, or seventieth trip, Stone fell to his knees on the hill and couldn't move. His eyes fixed on the ground in a half trance, he sensed a figure ahead. It was Chama, standing directly in his way.

"Enough, Martin Stone," she said firmly. "You are passing from the realm of making yourself strong into the realm of damaging your muscles, your tendons. You seem like an intelligent, strong man, Martin. But you are also a child, a fool, playing dark games with yourself. We Utes have a saying: Do what you do, complete your destiny—but do it with all your being. If you are a rabbit, run. If you are hawk, fly. If you are a warrior, you fight your enemy, not yourself, for a man is his only opponent, and once he has conquered himself none may defeat him. Do you understand, Martin Stone? Do you hear what I'm telling you?" she asked him, almost yelling, her soft eyes stormy and wild.

"Yes, I hear—but I must keep going. I don't even know why I just—"

"Then get past this," Chama yelled, pulling out a large hunting knife that hung on her right hip. "Because I don't want to have to be the one to bury you when your heart explodes from pushing yourself like a locomotive."

"All right," Stone said, letting his shoulders fall. "I'm sure

as hell not going to fight you." She led him off to one of the smaller fires, where her clan within the tribe, consisting of uncles, nephews, and all the complex interweavings of Ute society, sat around in wolf and buffalo robes, laughing and telling stories to one another as they gobbled down the slabs of meat from the elk leg that a boy was turning on a long spit over the flames. Chama reached forward and sliced two thick pieces off with her blade and sat down beside Martin on a log near the fire, handing him the bigger piece.

He had just finished his third piece, along with three thick slices of corn bread the Indians had baked in long ceramic pans, when he heard the sound of yelling, screaming coming from the central fire some fifty yards off. Stone began to rise, startled by the noise, but Chama reached up and pulled him down.

"It's just the wolf ceremony beginning," she said. "Don't worry, it's a ritual dance my people perform to show respect for the gods. And to act out the sacred myths of the rebirth of my tribe after the war." Stone reseated himself and watched through the cool night air as Ute braves assembled around the fire in a circle. They wore costumes made from the hides of wolves, elk, moose, beaver—all the inhabitants of the Rocky Mountains—complete with heads and tails and legs with paws still on them. Martin watched in fascination. There were nearly a hundred of the animal men stretching around the roaring flames into which other Utes were heaving wood, making it rise fifteen, twenty feet into the air in sheets of showering sparks.

Drums broke the crackling and popping of the fire with pounding deep rhythms as otherworldly as the thunder growling down from the storm-threatening skies above. Stone felt

the very bones of his body vibrate in response to the sounds. The braves began circling the fire about ten feet from its outer edge in a chanting line of hides and claws.

Martin had seen cowboy-and-Indian movies on TV—what American boy hadn't?—had seen them shot from their horses as they surrounded wagon trains, had seen them perform their primitive dances. But on screen they had seemed ridiculous, parodies of themselves. Here, though, as the Ute braves moved with animal grace, their war-painted faces and their unbridled screams up at the heavens demanding the attention of the gods, they appeared far from mockeries. They were the primeval force, the primal scream of man, searching for his place in the universe through mystery and magic rather than by way of spread sheet and data-base frame. The roaring fire, the undulating pelts atop the braves' backs, the mixed scents of animal musk and human sweat, the shooting stars streaming across the sky, burning tunnels through the clouds—all made it feel to Stone as if he were witnessing a ceremony from the dawn of time.

A palpable energy seemed to fill the air—the presence of something not quite human. The wind picked up and the branches off in the surrounding woods began shaking and clawing at the air. Stone felt a trembling sensation deep in his gut, as if he were seeing something he shouldn't, a bridge being built to another dimension, as if the distinction between man and beast, between earth and heaven were blurring and melting into one. The animal-clad figures circled faster and the drums increased their speed, taut copper arms slamming down like pistons onto tightly stretched skins.

Suddenly the entire circle stopped in its tracks. Martin's head snapped to the right as he saw a figure running from

out of the gnarled shadows of the wind-whipped woods. Goosepimples rose on his ice-cold arms, for the thing looked like a ghost—glowing, moving as if floating above the ground. But as it drew closer, Stone saw that it was one of the Muache, his face covered with white powder and wearing a tattered mock-up of a business suit. Feeling suddenly very uncomfortable, Stone realized what animal this brave was simulating—a white man, a white demon—one of those who had brought on the Great Fires.

He walked with a jerking, zombielike gait, as if half dead, stamping his legs down on the soil, reaching out with stiff arms for the living. The white-faced demon tore into the Utes still frozen in midstride, knocking them down, smashing apart the circle of harmony as he weaved drunkenly around the entire circumference of the fire. When he had completed one full circle, all the animals lay on the ground motionless, dead.

The white demon raised its arms to the flames, as if thanking them, and took a fist-sized pouch from his side. With all his strength he threw the object into the center of the fire and rushed backward. The pouch soared in an arc and fell into the very heart of the bonfire. There was a loud puff, not really an explosion, and a funnel of thick black smoke rose like a striking snake into the sky. Within seconds the entire village was blocked from the heavens as the smoke rushed up and formed something approximating a mushroom cloud stretching up in a boiling mountain five hundred feet above their heads.

Stone's eyes teared up as the downward drafts of the pungent smoke blew into his face. But he couldn't stop looking with spellbound fascination at the Ute tribe's ritual reenactment of World War III. The white demon leaped around the

perimeter of the fire, jumping high in the air as the mushroom cloud hung above him like the dark soil about to be shoveled on a corpse. It seemed happy, ecstatic that all had been destroyed, and it danced over the corpses of the fallen animals with a greatly exaggerated smile on its red-rouged lips. For just a split second, Stone saw the thing looking at him, and he could swear that its corpselike eyes were picking him out of the crowd, accusing, hating.

Suddenly one of the Utes at its feet—a wolf—began rising, unsteadily at first as it seemed wounded, but it shook itself, let out a roar, and began stalking the white man. Then a bear-clad figure rose, then a moose and a cougar until the white figure was fleeing for its life, pursued by the entire pack of snarling, clawing beasts. Within seconds they caught up with it and covered the creature like an army of hunter ants. The white demon threw its arms over its face, let out a scream, and then it was gone.

The Utes carried out the mock ritual of ripping the fallen creature's flesh apart, each taking a bite of it. Then they began dancing around the fire again, the mushroom cloud at last dissipating as the north wind sent it swirling off to every point of the compass. The drums started up faster, making the braves race around the fire to keep time with them. The Muache throughout the village rose from their log seats and came forward. Young and old alike, from strong young braves to leather-faced elders hardly able to walk, all headed to the bonfire, where they formed their own second circle around the animal circle revolving within. They spun the opposite way, jumping, dancing in a mad ecstasy, in a pure and unequivocal celebration of life.

Stone watched with a kind of awe at the free and open

way the Utes expressed their joy at being alive, at the way they showed how man and animal and nature must live together so that they could all survive. If the Caucasian race had had such an understanding and respect for life, perhaps things would have been different. He cursed his race for having become technological geniuses who hadn't understood their relationship to this planet worth a damn, hadn't understood that what seemed immutable to them—their very civilization—was in fact just one of many evolutionary experiments of nature. And the test tube containing mankind was about to be poured down the drain.

CHAPTER SEVEN

After about half an hour, the ritual ended and the members of the tribe went back to their respective fires. Wolf and elk skins dropped from sweat-covered shoulders to the ground, and the braves walked among each other, laughing and rubbing their hands over their chests to dry them. They sat down off to one side of the raging fire and began a different sort of ritual—that of pure strength, of one man against another. Two Utes stripped to their deerskin loincloths and grappled with one another in the center of a black circle fifteen feet in diameter. They moved slowly at first and then with bursts of sudden power. At last one of them threw his opponent out of the circle. He raised his arms in victory, and another brave rose from the crowd to try his skill.

Stone stood up and started toward the hundred or so braves seated on the cold soil as they cheered their favorite on.

"Don't," Chama said, grabbing his arm. But he just lifted

her hand from his wrist and walked forward. If he had nothing else, it was still his country too—he'd walk where he wanted. Numerous eyes glanced his way as he walked until he was standing about thirty feet behind the seated warriors. They didn't seem too happy that the white man was among them, but apparently there was some sort of etiquette about visitors to the village, and not one raised his voice toward Stone, or his fist.

He took in the Utes' fighting style with interest. The years he had spent in the shelter learning fighting techniques from his father had made him quite knowledgeable about different styles, throws, strikes. The Utes were strong, quick, moving with the speed of the animals they had just imitated. But they fought more with pride, with dramatic explosions of power— trying to lift the other man by the leg or up over the shoulders and fling him from the ring—than with the many maneuvers that the human body was capable of. Stone couldn't help but wonder how he would do against them. All that he had learned had been in controlled circumstances—this was a little more real. The veins of his strong young body suddenly coursed with excitement as he imagined the countermoves he would make.

The Utes fought for nearly two hours, the winner of each clash staying in the circle until he was tossed out—and then the next. At last there were just two of them left—the brave in the center of the black circle and his opponent, a good seven feet tall, with a necklace of coyote teeth around his bull-sized neck. Stone could see from the way the huge fellow strode into the ring of combat that he was the one the Utes had been waiting for—the tough guy of the tribe with that unconcerned, almost bored expression of a man who knows

he cannot be beaten. He walked toward his stocky opponent with muscles rippling along his body like steel cables about to pop, and the two began to grapple. The giant didn't waste a second playing around. He wished all to see his full strength, for these were contests but not games. Slipping one hamhock-sized hand around the brave's thigh, he lifted the man straight up until he was holding him above his head and threw him out of the circle. The brave hit the dirt and rolled over several times, rising beaten but unhurt.

The winner snorted and turned slowly around so that all could see his strength, his massive physique, his eyes darting here and there to see if there were any further challengers tonight. But none rose. The giant's eyes passed over Martin, stopping for a second, and then moved on. Stone felt something come over him, something he had never felt before in his life—the desire to show his strength, to get up there and knock the man down. Without really knowing what he was doing, as if following some hidden commands of his subconscious, the six-foot 180-pound twenty-three-year-old rose and walked toward the Ute who outweighed him nearly two to one.

All eyes turned toward him. It was like being met with a solid wall of hate, of disgust and loathing. But Martin kept his gaze firm. It was time to test himself, see what he was really made of. He would sure as hell need to know if he was going to survive in this twisted world.

"You do woman's work," the giant laughed out with contempt, looking down at the flea who approached him. "I do not fight women."

"Tell you what, fatso," Stone said, hardly believing his own words. "I'm going to kick your ass. How about that?"

Deep in his chest Martin could feel all the accumulated rage and anger he had bottled up rising up in him like a poisonous bile that had to be released or it would destroy him. He had been picked on too much—first by his father, then the murdering slime who had killed his mother and sister and nearly him. Every man has his breaking point, and Stone had reached his—the borderline between childhood and manhood, an instant in which one reaches down and there is something different inside, something that will not accept another wound, mental or physical. Stone stepped into that doorway unsure if he would come through the other side.

The Utes hadn't spoken English for years—it was the forbidden language, the tongue of the Destroyer. But they understood his words, and Stone could hear the gasps at his challenge. The giant's face twisted up in anger which, as he realized he was about to get the opportunity to smash the white bug, turned into a slash of a smile oozing malevolence. He motioned with a finger the size of an ear of corn for Stone to come forward. Without a moment's hesitation Martin walked through the outer edge of the coal-black circle. If the Utes thought he was going to use hit-and-run speed, which was their basic approach to the top tough boy, they were wrong. He moved straight ahead, neither rushing nor cringing at the sight of the bronzed figure with arms as large as his challenger's legs. Somehow Martin was right in front of him before the seven-footer had a chance to react, as he was still smirking and shaking his head in mock pity for the benefit of his Ute audience.

The tree-sized arms suddenly rose and then descended, reaching for the impudent ant, while the Ute's eyes filled with a dark, unreflecting light that spoke of no mercy but

imminent death. But as the human battering rams dropped, Stone simply extended his right arm straight out and up, driving the blade of his hand into the Ute's throat just above the apple-sized Adam's apple. The tough boy looked suddenly surprised, his eyes popping wide so that the whites above and below showed. He couldn't understand for a few seconds what was happening to him, as he hadn't experienced pain for quite a number of years. None had been able to hurt him. But suddenly he remembered and slammed both immense hands over his throat, gasping for air as his trachea squashed shut like a hose that's just been stepped on.

He wheezed out violently and then sucked in just as hard, his face growing beet-red, the veins in his neck and eyes standing out from their fleshy soil like vines trying to rise. Whatever thoughts the Ute fighter had about taking Martin down vanished in the sudden terror that he himself was about to die. Stone saw his opportunity and reached forward with his hand again formed into a spear, the fingers held tightly together. He placed his hand dead center on the oversized Ute's abdomen and pushed hard. So off balance was the brave as he held his throat as if strangling himself that Stone was able to just push the four hundred plus pounds of humanity straight backward as if he were a weightless balloon. At the very edge of the circle, Stone simply extended his arm and the giant tumbled over like a great tree, its roots finally snapped, and fell backward onto the ground.

The entire assemblage, which just seconds before had been cheering the white man's destruction, grew dead silent as they watched with obvious displeasure Stone's easy victory over their champion.

"Shit," he muttered under his breath as, head down, he

turned and started walking away. He'd fucked up again—alienated the very people who'd saved his damned ass. Everything he did seemed to end up causing pain for him and others. He felt cursed.

"Stop!" a voice yelled out from the crowd of Utes. Startled, Martin turned and searched for the source. A brave walked to the front of the seated Muache. He was stark naked, with black and green stripes painted lengthwise up his body. On his head sat an immense headdress of feathers and bones that draped over his shoulders and down his back. His entire face was covered with red dots, each the size of a quarter, that appeared to have been tattooed right into the flesh. As he spoke, Stone could see that his teeth had been filed into points, giving him a canine and quite nightmarish appearance.

"You fight well, white man," the Ute vision right out of a Bosch painting said. "I'm sure my people here think it was a mistake and doubtless would like their hero to try again. But my eyes see deeper into the nature of things, and I can tell that you are a powerful warrior. How did one so young learn such deadly skills?" Stone was flabbergasted that the Stone Age–looking thing before him spoke with perfect diction, enunciating each word as if he were reciting a Shakespearean sonnet.

"I—I—learned from my father, Major Clayton R. Stone. He was a commando, a warrior of the old days. But, you—who are you? You speak English so well."

"I am Ouray, the shaman—medicine man I believe is what the Caucasian books would call me." He laughed out loud, a low, sobbing laugh that made the hair rise on Stone's arms, for it sounded more animal than human—like the half laugh, half howl that one might hear the wolves pouring out from

their mountain homes in the darkest hour of the night. He was from another world, another age. "But I use no medicine," Ouray went on, moving slowly forward toward Stone. "At least none that you would recognize—no pills, no ointments or hypodermics. My medicines have to do with the gods—with the screams of the wind and the claws of the moon. I am the holder of secrets, the giver of ways out."

"Ways out?" Stone asked nervously as the Ute shaman came right up to him and stopped a foot away. He stared directly into Martin's face, and the younger man could barely take the energy, the power emanating from those impenetrable orbs. The eyes seemed completely black, without a centimeter of white in them, like dark jewels created in a cave so deep in the earth they could not give off a sliver of light. And from only inches away Stone could see the myriad scars that filled the man's face—self-inflicted gouges of sacred symbols—moons, skulls, miniature wolves, mountain lions, knives, snakes—all carved into the red skin so that as the flickering light of the bonfire reflected off of it the face seemed almost alive, its magical artwork appearing to move around it.

Stone rubbed his eyes as the flesh paintings began to hypnotize him, make him dizzy. He stepped back. He sensed the man had powers over other men, abilities far beyond the norm. Yet he did not feel in danger. Somehow there was a directness, an honesty that he had never encountered before.

"Do not fear me, Martin Stone," the shaman said. "*I* am not the one who will hurt you. But if you have courage beyond anything you have ever had before, I will show you the way out."

"You keep saying that," Martin said, annoyed, as he tried

to hide—even from himself—the fact that he was afraid. He could feel it—energy streaming around the man—see it at the edges of the shadows that streaked up and down the shaman's painted body. "Way out, way out—the way out of what?"

"The way out of anything, Stone," Ouray said, laughing again so that his mouth opened wide and the two rows of canine teeth were in full view. "The way out of here, the way out of your guilt, the way to the ghosts of your mother and sister."

"How do you know all these things about me?" Stone asked nervously. "About my feelings, my sister?"

"Thoughts are like birds, Stone. You have merely to watch them fly, see their trajectories to know where they are going. Come with me if you wish to find answers. If you can fight as well inside as out." The shaman turned without waiting to see the white man's response and walked through the seated crowd of Utes, who parted like water as he passed. Hardly knowing why, Stone followed along behind. His life had seemed like a dream from the moment he and his family had left the shelter—a dream of death and blood. Perhaps this witch doctor, or whatever the hell he was, knew the way out—the way to a better dream.

The shaman walked through the darkness and up a slope at the edge of the village into the woods. Martin followed about ten yards behind, just able to see the man's glistening, tattoo-covered body from the light of the towering fire behind them. But within minutes, as they climbed higher and higher into the trees, the illuminating rays of the flames disappeared and it was all Stone could do to keep up with the man as he stumbled on the gravel-strewn mountainside. They must have

walked for half an hour at full speed, the shaman not even bothering to glance around, for he knew the white man was there as he knew the stars and the moon lay above him.

At last they reached a small plateau devoid of trees. The shaman made his way straight for a round wooden platform, with six other Utes similarly clad in skin and paint seated around it. Above each of them was a tripod of branches extending about ten feet above their heads, tied together at the top. He joined them and motioned for Martin to do the same. The six began chanting, a low, almost inaudible sound, the sound of wind rustling through thick leaves. Ouray, seated directly across from Martin, spoke to him softly but distinctly.

"Listen to what I say, Stone, for every word could mean your life—now and in the future, if there is one." Stone looked around for a second, and the view made him catch his breath. They were high on a mountain peak of the central Rockies. The clouds had dissipated completely now, blown apart by the arctic winds beginning their nightly howling across the range, and the stars shone down by the trillions, lighting up the pine-blanketed mountains that stretched off to the horizon as far as the eye could see. If the idea of the ritual Stone was about to take part in was to make him feel small in the eyes of God, to make him less than a mite contrasted against the beauty of the purple mountains' majesty—it had already succeeded.

"Ten thousand years ago my people came here," Ouray said as his disciples' droning chant continued around them. "We came from the Asias, where the snows were too harsh, the warring tribes too mad in their desire to conquer and destroy all the others. We came here—the first to America. The first humans. But there were others then. More horrible,

murderous than anything you could dream up in your imag-
ination. Demon men, ghouls, drinkers of human blood. Those
were days of magic, days of legend.

"We fought then to conquer this new world. And many
Indians died. From the Ute, the Navajo, the Apache tribes.
We fought the last of the old world, destroyed it so that the
new one could come into being. And for a thousand years it
was so—the Indians shared the land and the buffalo and lived
at peace, one with all. It was a way that the rest of civilization
might have tried. But Western man forgot his heart, his soul,
as if such things being invisible, unmarketable, didn't matter,
and cared only for the machine, the war machine. And he
has won, Martin Stone. His machines have carried out their
ultimate goal and fought a war that has broken down whatever
so-called civilization there was into little poisoned clumps,
groups of murderers and barbarians that have sunk to such
depths of depravity and cruelty to their fellow man that—I
fear—the blackness, the demons of the human soul, the disease that rots all that is noble in a man, in a society until all
that is left is the pure desire to hurt, to harm others, the
essence of sadism, a fascism of the human soul—has returned. A state of decay has come again that will send the
world plunging into a dark age from which it will not again
emerge." He paused to see if Martin was taking it all in,
fixing his eyes on him like a fox on a chicken.

"I—I hear you," Martin managed to mumble, "though I'm
not quite sure, to be honest with you, what you're trying to
tell me."

"The ancient days are here again, Martin Stone. The final
war for the survival of mankind as a species has begun. And
it was said in the old days that there would arise among men

a few warriors with the power, the ability to fight back. Just a few, and they would barely have a chance against the darkness that lay out there. But they would go anyway, Stone, for it would be their fate to go. You are one of those men. The Nadi, we call them—those with the gift of bestowing death."

"I don't know if that's a gift I want," Stone said.

"It's yours whether you desire it or not," the shaman spat out between his canine teeth, showing their pointed tips again, as if his jaws might snap out at any moment and take a bite out of Stone's face. Martin wondered whether those jaws had ever closed around a human throat—and suddenly somehow knew that they had.

CHAPTER
EIGHT

The shaman clapped his hands with a loud crack that startled Stone. The others stopped chanting and opened their eyes wide. One of them reached forward for a bowl that sat at the edge of the glowing coals and, hefting it toward his mouth, took a deep gulp of the contents. The steaming bowl was handed around the circle until it reached Martin.

"Take it," the shaman commanded. "Drink it."

"What the hell is it?" Stone asked, looking down at the foul-smelling green soup inside.

"Peyote—the sacred mescal that links us with the wolf and the bear gods. The plant that divines the truth. Drink it!"

Stone lifted it slowly to his lips, took a deep gulp of the stuff, and nearly vomited. It was the worst thing he had ever tasted, like the vomit of skid row, the rot and mildew that stank under every log. But somehow he kept it down, his eyes fixed on the cool white snows capping the mountains

all around him, imagining himself drinking their freezing, numbing liquid.

The peyote stew slinked its way down toward his stomach, and he could feel its heat inside him. The others began chanting again, their eyes fixed on the bleached buffalo skull set in the middle of the wood platform on a pole. Within minutes Stone began feeling the effects. It was not unpleasant at first—a kind of rubbery feeling around the joints and face, as if everything could just be stretched out like taffy. He felt all his cells relaxing, sinking down into him as the Indian drug flowed through his veins.

"Hey, that's not bad," Stone half giggled, looking over at Ouray with a ridiculous smile. The shaman ignored the words, his face and body as still as set concrete, and Stone, once again realizing he was breaking the rules, shut up. He looked up, his eye caught by the motion of something high in the sky. A meteor streaked across the black ocean of the sky, disappearing in the far mountains, but Stone kept staring at the trail of the hot rock, which seemed to hang in the sky like the smoke from a jet engine. He turned his head, and the world streaked and bled together, every object in his sight leaving a hundred afterimages behind it which took seconds to vanish, like the images left on a television screen when it's turned off.

The entire universe suddenly burst into motion, the skies a swirling waterfall of galaxies and nebulas shooting down a trillion beams of light that seemed to come straight for him across the light-years separating them. He shifted his eyes to the near woods, and here too it was as if he were looking into another dimension—one not seen by normal vision. He could see every needle on the pine trees, the owls sitting high

in the branches scanning the hills below for the sudden motion that meant food. It was as if he were part of it all and knew what everything felt.

He had no idea how long he was in the melting lushness of vision and sensation that flowed from everywhere like golden honey onto his senses, but suddenly he was snapped back in by the shaman's barking voice.

"Yes, it is good, is it not, Martin Stone?" Ouray asked, his black eyes now glowing from within with a green light, his scarred flesh seeming to undulate before Martin's huge, dilated pupils. "But that is only one edge of the night. The beautiful side. There is another side—the darkness, the opposition, the evil. For that is what awaits you out there. Are you ready?"

"It's your show, pal," Stone answered, wondering what the hell was going to happen next. But he didn't have to wait long to find out. The Ute's magic men rose to their feet and backed off until each was standing just beneath one of the wooden tripods above him. They pulled down the ropes that were attached to the top, and as Stone looked on with a sinking feeling in his guts, they put the narrow bone spikes at the ends through their outer chest muscles, pushing right through the painted flesh as if slicing through the Sunday roast. Thin trickles of blood ran out between their fingers and down their chests, covering them with an instant sheen of red.

The shaman stood below the tripod next to Martin's and, eyes fixed on the younger man, he pushed the sharp daggers through his skin without batting an eyelash. Stone reached up and grabbed hold of his two ropes and pulled them down to chest level. The peyote was hitting him in waves now, and he was afraid he was going to vomit everything he had eaten

in the last twenty-four hours all over the platform. But somehow he held it down and pulled his khaki jacket open, lifting the sweat shirt beneath it. He placed the cold tip of the engraved staghorn spike against his right chest and pushed hard sideways. The pain was tremendous, like a trail of burning napalm sweeping through the nerves and veins of his entire upper body, but he knew that the eyes of the whole powwow were on him and he didn't flinch. Then he pushed the other one through, which seemed to snag somehow on the outer sheathing of muscle. With a quick exhale, he rammed it forward and it too pierced the flesh and came out several inches over. The shaman looked around to make sure the rest of the assistant magic makers were all hooked up nice and tight and then looked back at Martin.

"Look into your soul, Martin Stone. Do it now so that when you go out into the darkness you know who you are. Only those who burn with their own light can remain untouched by the storm of death. Know yourself, Stone. Who are you? Who are you?" In his peyote-heightened state, the words seemed to echo through Martin's brain like thunder rolling through the mountains. What did he mean, who are you? He was . . . he was . . . He searched and suddenly couldn't find himself in the kaleidoscope of color around him, in the melting of the trees and the oceanic swells and falls of the leaf- and pine-needle-covered plateau. The shaman suddenly reached forward toward a wooden lever just in front of him and without warning pulled it hard. Trapdoors beneath all the men dropped open, and they fell into the space, the bone spikes ripping up into their chests so that they bounced up and down, held only by their own flesh.

Stone fell only a few inches, but it felt like a mile as his

muscles and outer flesh stretched up from his body to take
the weight of the rest of him. The pain was so instantaneous
and all-consuming that he felt as if all he was was a bundle
of torturous sensations—a thing without a name other than
pain. He dangled there for minutes, trying not to scream out
as his eyes filled with moisture, but not a tear fell. Somehow
even in his mindlessness he knew this was a test whose rules
he had no concept of but which he could not fail. He opened
his eyes, and the light of the stars filled his supersensitive
pupils with floodlights so intense that he winced and pulled
his head involuntarily back, jarring the spikes in his chest,
making the nerves scream out harshly in electric jolts that ran
through his heart and spine like a spasm with teeth. Somehow
he stilled himself, suspended there in the air, and moving
only his eyes he looked at the others. Every one of them was
staring at the bleached buffalo head which sat dead center of
the platform, staring back on them all through its empty eye
sockets through which the galaxies on high seemed to pour
in a waterfall of ice.

"Jesus God," Stone muttered involuntarily at the sight, not
even realizing he had spoken. As if answering, the wind
suddenly picked up with a roar as if a fleet of tanks were
driving through the forests. The branches bent and leaves
flew. The wind tore into the men hanging like slabs of beef
and swung them wildly around like puppets on strings of fire.

HE WAS ONLY PAIN. ALL THAT HIS CELLS WERE
COMPOSED OF WAS PAIN. HE COULD FEEL THE CIR-
CLES OF STABBING NUMBNESS SPREAD OUT FROM
THE SPIKES THAT PIERCED HIM AND RIPPLE DOWN
THROUGH EVERY MOLECULE OF HIM, LEAVING NOT
A STONE UNTOUCHED. HE SEARCHED BUT

COULDN'T FIND HIS FEET, HIS HANDS. HE WAS NO LONGER A BEING WITH PARTS BUT JUST A MEDIUM FOR THE MESSAGE OF TORTURE. THE BUFFALO HEAD SEEMED TO GLOW WITH THE SAME DARK GREEN FIRE AS THE SHAMAN'S EYES, AND STONE FELT HIMSELF FALLING TOWARD THE EYE SOCK-ETS, FALLING AS IF FOREVER. HE WAS IN THE BONY EYE HOLES, WITH THE TERMITES AND WORMS CRAWLING AROUND THEIR FADED EDGES. HE WAS ONE OF THE BUGS. JUST A SLIME THING OOZING ALONG ON A TRAIL OF STICKY MUCUS, SEARCHING FOR DRIED FLECKS OF FLESH.

SUDDENLY THE PEYOTE HIT INTO STONE IN A TIDAL WAVE AS ALL HIS SENSES MIXED TO-GETHER—SOUND, SIGHT, TASTE, TOUCH—SO HE NO LONGER KNEW WHERE HE ENDED AND WHERE THE SKULL BEGAN. THE SKULL EXPLODED INTO A THOUSAND SKULLS, AND THEY FELL ONTO THE DIRT, IMPLANTING THEMSELVES IN THE HARD GROUND. FROM OUT OF THE EYES AND THE CRACKED SLOTS WHERE THE EARS HAD ONCE BEEN MAGGOTS BEGAN SPEWING FORTH IN GREAT AR-MIES—ENDLESS NUMBERS OF THEM. THEY CAME ACROSS THE PLATFORM TOWARD STONE AND THE OTHERS. HE FELT THEM ON HIS FOOT AND THEN HIS LEG, FELT THEIR TINY WET JAWS DIGGING IN, SLICING OUT PARTS OF HIM.

SUDDENLY FROM THE GROUND AROUND THE LU-MINESCENT WHITE BUFFALO HEADS HANDS BURST FORTH FROM THE SOIL. HUMAN HANDS, OR WHAT HAD ONCE BEEN HUMAN. THEY CLAWED AND DUG

THEIR WAY UP FURIOUSLY, AND STONE, NOT EVEN KNOWING WHO OR WHERE HE WAS, FELT THE MASS OF NAUSEA THAT HAD BEEN HIS STOMACH BEGIN TO RUMBLE AS IF PREPARING TO SEND UP A STREAM OF HOT BILE. THE HANDS BROKE FREE, AND HE COULD SEE THAT THEY WERE BURNT AND DRIPPING, COVERED WITH PUS-FILLED SORES AND BLISTERS THAT POPPED EVEN AS THEY MOVED, STREAMING DOWN OVER HIS FINGERS, RELEASING A RIVER THAT SLUGS AND MULTILEGGED SUCKERS CRAWLING ALONG THE BODIES DRANK DOWN, ATTACHING THEMSELVES AROUND THE WOUNDS LIKE LEECHES.

THE DEAD ROSE IN STATES OF WRETCHED DECAY, WITH PURPLE FACES AND TONGUES SWOLLEN OUT LIKE THICK SNAKES CRAWLING FROM THEIR MOUTHS. THEY STARTED TOWARD STONE, REACHING FOR HIM, LICKING THEIR BLACK LIPS TOGETHER WITH GHASTLY RIPPING SOUNDS AS THE ROTTING FLESH TORE RIGHT OUT OF THEIR MOUTHS.

"JESUS, JESUS," STONE WHISPERED UNDER HIS BREATH OVER AND OVER LIKE SOME SORT OF PROTECTIVE MANTRA. AS IF SPEAKING INSIDE HIS SKULL, THE SHAMAN'S VOICE CAME TO HIM.

"THEY CANNOT HARM YOU IF YOU DO NOT WILL IT, MARTIN STONE. THEY ARE THE DEAD SOULS FROM THE WAR. THE DEAD SOULS OF MODERN AMERICA, THE WOUNDED AND MURDERED WHO ARE CREATED EACH DAY BY THE SAVAGES, THE ENEMIES OF MAN WHO RULE. SEE THEM, FACE

THEM, FOR THIS IS YOUR ENEMY—THE GHOULS, THE DEFILERS, MEN WITH DEAD HEARTS WHO FEAST ON THEIR BROTHERS AND SISTERS JUST AS THESE DEAD DO. WHO ARE YOU, MARTIN STONE? WHEN YOU KNOW—THEN YOU WILL KNOW HOW TO FIGHT THEM."

BUT THE THINGS CAME FORWARD UNTIL THEY WERE ALMOST UPON HIM, HANDS REACHING, BLOOD SPLATTERED, AND TORN FINGERNAILS SLICING TOWARD HIM. HE SAW THE FACES OF THE TWO CLOSEST ONES AND HE SCREAMED, FOR IT WAS HIS FATHER AND MOTHER. THEY WERE HIDEOUS, DARK CARICATURES OF HIS REAL PARENTS, THEIR TEETH ROTTING BLACK STUMPS THAT DANGLED AT ODD ANGLES IN THEIR PALE MOUTHS. THEIR EYES HAD TURNED TO CLAY AND WERE HARD AND UNSEEING INSIDE PURPLE SOCKETS. THEY SMILED AT HIM.

"MARTIN, MARTIN, WE'VE COME TO GET YOU. YOU'LL LIVE WITH US. WE LOVE YOU, MARTIN. WE WANT YOU WITH US. WE'LL BE TOGETHER AGAIN. YOU'LL LIKE IT BELOW. IT'S SO COLD AND HARD. COME, MARTIN, COME WITH US." THEY REACHED FOR HIM.

"NO," STONE SCREAMED, PUSHING AT THEM WITH HIS FISTS, WHICH SENT MORE JOLTS OF EXQUISITE LIGHTNING THROUGH HIS CHEST MUSCLES. BUT SUDDENLY THE LIGHTNING ARCED UP AND OUT OF HIS BODY AND INTO THE CORPSE PARENTS, KNOCKING THEIR HEADS FROM THEIR BODIES AS BLACK, ROTTING INNARDS SPOUTED UP FROM THE NECKS.

THEY MELTED INTO A STEAMING PILE OF BUB-
BLING OIL. AND WERE GONE. GONE FOREVER.

He was back, hanging in the air, the sudden awareness of
the burning pain in his chest a welcome relief from the hellish
vision he had just seen. Yet he felt free. Free for the first
time. Free from the confines of his family, from the guilt of
their deaths. He hadn't killed them. They were all brought
into this world with their own fates to carry out. Theirs had
been to die, his to live. He was alone now. And strangely,
he felt a secret joy in it.

He hung on the ropes through the night as the others too
swung back and forth, buffeted by the winds, each going
through his own secret hell—enlightenment, Ute style. He
hardly felt the pain now, his eyes calm with the knowledge
that he had faced the worst thing he could know on this earth
and had survived. No man, no living or dead thing would
ever frighten him again. Martin Stone was reborn out of pain
and terror into something called a man.

CHAPTER NINE

As the dawn sun crawled on feeble yellow legs into the indigo sky, its pale rays fell on seven men dangling in the air, their faces set in strange masks somewhere between ecstasy and agony. The shaman pulled the lever again, and the trapdoors swung back up into place so the men were able to once again stand on their feet. They pulled the spikes from their chests and passed around a gourd that had been sitting near the coals. It was filled with warm mud. Ouray motioned for the white man to slap it over the bleeding red holes on his chest, which Martin did. Within seconds the stinging pain vanished and was replaced by a soothing heat which permeated down to his chilled bones.

In total silence the eight travelers into the human soul left the platform, not to return again for a year, and headed back down the mountain to the village whose thin breaths of wispy smoke they could see far below. From the crevices and un-

reachable caverns that had been wind-carved into the sheer granite above them, eagles jumped forward into the morning air, spreading their golden wings out wide as if they were gliding on feathers of fire. The great birds of prey noticed the band of humans but knew they posed no danger and soared past them, barely moving a feather as they caught the thermal updrafts from below. They moved only their reptilian heads sharply back and forth, searching the woods below for early morning creatures out foraging for roots and nuts.

Not one man said a word. What is there to say after a man has seen into the very core of his soul? Stone was in a daze. He felt different. New. But when he reached for the change with his mind, it was intangible. Yet he knew he had changed. He felt older, filled with the cold wisdom that comes from a lifetime of experience and suffering. Yet those years, that self-knowledge had been given to him in a single night. All the self-hatred, the guilt that had filled him to overflowing were gone. He didn't know where, and he didn't want to know. But he was thankful. He was ready to face whatever was out there, ready to start down the road to his destiny, a highway that he knew would be paved in an asphalt of blood.

They reached the village greeted by rib-poking, half-wild dogs that were the tribe's hunting partners and sometime pets. The skinny creatures came rushing at them, jumping frantic circles in the air before men they thought were returning hunters who would throw a scrap or two their way. But the shaman clapped his hand and looked fiercely down at the beggars, and they ran off whimpering, the power of the magic man apparent even to the animals. At last Martin saw his distinctive tent, with its two large if somewhat weathered

antlers on each side of the entrance, and headed in. He was asleep before his face hit the pungent bear-hide pillow.

Someone was touching him. He couldn't tell if it was a dream or real. His life seemed to be nothing but a dream now. But this dream was real. It smelled of woman, sweet vessel of intoxicating perfume which filled his nostrils with an urgent scent, bringing his desires to full bloom before the mind was fully awake.

"Martin," the shadow spoke. "I want you. I want you." The shape dropped its buckskin clothing and slid under the thick fur of what had once been a thousand-pound black bear and pressed her hot, naked body against Stone's. That woke him fully as his glands pumped out hormones that had been dormant for five years and his body trembled with sudden explosive desire.

"Chama, what—" he began.

"Shh," the Ute woman said, putting her fingers over his lips. "I've waited for you. Waited for the man worthy of taking me. You are the man. I give you my body, Martin Stone, my mouth and my breasts—and my opening, which no màn has ever laid eyes on or touched. Take it—do what you will with me. Make me a woman, a real woman who has had a man take her deep within."

She pressed herself against him, cleaving every square inch of her smooth copper body to his skin as if she were a blanket covering him. Her pear-sized breasts, firm and proud, pressed against his muscled chest, her nipples hard and red as cherries waiting to be plucked from their blood-flushed branches. Her lips kissed at his neck and then his cheeks over and over again like a small animal biting at him with mad affection. The moist lips at last found his and clamped down

on them, her tongue darting quickly in and out as his followed suit and filled her opened mouth.

He was still in somewhat of a daze from the peyote that still circulated in his veins. Her face, her skin seemed to glow with a warm translucence that was the sheer opposite of what he had just experienced. Death was the dark side—and this the light. Always the two went hand in hand. She was so beautiful it was almost painful, hard for him to look at. He had slept with girls before—before they had gone into the shelter. But this was different. The others had been teenage games—pawings, the snappings of pants and shirt buttons. This was a meeting of raw desires, of bodies filled with an ocean of longing ready to burst forth in a flood of animal lust. He reached down and grabbed her, pulling her hips hard against him. His manhood grew stiff and seemed to rise forever, reaching for her, filled with its own life and electricity.

He slid his right hand around her side and then between the two of them, searching until he found her center. The triangle of hair was black and fine like silk threads, and he grabbed it whole in his hands and squeezed hard, as if taking possession of her, showing his strength over her. She groaned aloud and spread her legs apart, her pink, fleshy lips spreading like sun-filled petals waiting for his touch. He moved his palm down along the slit of her and then pushed with his index finger into her. Again she groaned and threw her head back, rolling it slowly from side to side. She was wet inside, like a surging river, growing wetter as he pumped the finger.

She was ready. He rolled over on top of her, placing his strong thighs between hers as she pulled apart even farther, lifting her hips for him. Stone grabbed his pole of flesh, more

rigid than he had ever felt it, and dipped the swollen head into the jungle of hair and moistness below. Again she moaned with a guttural growl of raw desire that sent a wave of desire through Martin. He placed himself between the parted lips and leaned forward, grabbing her in a bear hug, crushing her breasts against him so that they were flat as pancakes, pulling her head into his neck.

With a single, powerful thrust he slammed forward and drove right through the little bit of virgin tissue that was left and into the deepest pit of her stomach. She screamed for just a second and then bit her teeth madly as she felt the thing inside her, the man organ, so big and taking up all of her. There was pain, but even as she breathed hard the sensation turned to pleasure as her muscles relaxed and the sheath of her molded like a glove around his staff of hardened flesh.

He waited a few seconds, letting her adjust to the length and thickness of him, and then began moving in and out of her. He went slowly at first, making sure she could keep up with him. Her mouth opened wider and wider, her eyes completely closed now as she felt only what he was doing to her down there, taking her mind, her soul into the pumping motion of his spear. She let her back sink deeper into the soft furs beneath them, arching her hips higher and higher, spreading her legs apart so as to make space for him, to open deeper as he pushed like a miner ever farther inside her.

He pulled her legs up around his back so that she seemed almost attached to him and began going hard now. He was without thought, without awareness of any kind except of her softness, into which he thrust himself again and again like the rain into the soil. She shook her head frantically from side to side now. Her body began to vibrate as if it would

take off. Suddenly, as if a dam had broken loose inside her, she reached up and grabbed hold of his hips and began pulling herself up against him, meeting each of his jackhammer thrusts with her own, slamming herself against him in convulsive, animal desperation.

They reached the top together, their breaths suddenly coming in harsh, quick intakes, and they screamed out simultaneously as the juices exploded out of each of them in pulsing orgasmic contractions while they continued to grind against one another as if trying to merge into one being.

They lay together, mindlessly stroking one another's flesh in a state of perfect peace. The low, flickering flames of the nearly burnt-out fire in the center of the tepee revealed little, quick snatches of each other's bodies—her sweat-covered breasts still pushed out hard, the nipples erect and trembling, his strong arms and veiny hands tracing circles around the stringy mat of her wet hair below.

"Martin Stone," she said at last, with much hesitancy. "You have given me what I have wanted. I must give you the same. Though I know it will take you from me by the morning's light, still, because I love you, I cannot lie to you. Your—your sister is alive."

Martin pulled suddenly away from her, forcing the bear rug over his back to fall onto the hard-packed, frigid ground below. "What do you mean—she's alive? They were killed at the attack. I saw them—"

"No, you saw your mother die. Your sister was attacked, but she wasn't killed. The Guardians of Hell took her. One of the braves who found you—he told me. They found only the two you killed and your mother. Your sister was captured. They will use her for their pleasure. They are always in need

of more women—the ones they have tend to get used up in a hurry."

"But where . . . where would they have taken her?" Stone asked, the calmness he had felt just seconds before, the brief state of happiness, the only such moments he had experienced in many years already gone into memory's files, where experience is downgraded to the level of thought and loses its beauty.

"To Denver," Chama said softly, her eyes looking down at the darkness of the space between them. "That is where their headquarters in these parts are. They control the whole city—what's left of it. They'll use her as one of their whores. If she's lucky, she'll be taken by one of their leaders and used only by him. If she's unlucky, she'll be put into one of their street houses—where she won't last long. Don't be angry at me, Martin," she pleaded, not wanting to lose the paradise they had just inhabited, needing his arms around her again. Tears began falling in her eyes as she realized she had ruined everything for herself, and she fell back on the bed in a heap.

"All right, it's all right," Stone said, coming out of his momentary shock. "I'm not mad—not at you. You and your people have been like family to me—a hell of a lot nicer than I'm sure my people would be under similar circumstances. I feel as if I've been reborn, lived a second life here. But—I've got to go. You know that."

"I know," she said, squeezing close to him again, her face breaking into a secret smile of reprieve. "Just make love to me again. Once more, before you go. The first made me a woman, the second will be the memory that I will hold inside my heart."

He left in the early afternoon just as the first of a band of

ominous-looking storm clouds began moving in from the north. With just the clothes he had taken from the shelter—jeans, a green sweat shirt, and a thick surplus Army fatigue jacket along with a blanket and a long, double-edged hunting blade that Chama gave him for protection—Stone headed out from the village. Only she and the shaman watched him go. They stood side by side, as motionless as the mountains that rose into the clouds above. Neither waved or said a word. But their eyes bespoke seas of emotion.

CHAPTER TEN

Martin Stone was alone for the first time in five years. It was a strange feeling. He and his family had been claustrophobically on top of one another in the shelter to the point of mutual suffocation. Then had come the attack, followed by the presence of the Utes all around him. But now, as he walked downslope into the thickening forests, he was completely, unalterably alone—a single moving figure in a mountain range that could be seen from the moon.

He had no plan other than to find his sister and get her out of whatever filthy hellhole she was in. But not like this. Not with just the knife on his hip. Not against an army of the bastards without his own equalizers. He'd have to get back to the shelter, arm himself, and then go to Denver. Everything he did from now on would have to be planned, thought out. There could be no more mistakes or he would just be throwing his life away. He felt the child in him, the

moody adolescent, the impetuous, emotional side of his nature slipping farther away by the second. And in his eyes was a new vision that made the world around him appear crystal clear, every pearl of ice hanging from every branch visible and glowing like a beacon through the freezing air.

He checked his pocket compass every half hour or so, heading toward the interstate, the location of which Chama had told him was about twenty miles due south. The going wasn't too bad at first, his body keeping him warm as long as he kept moving, his mouth puffing out little spouts of white with every exhale. But by evening, as the beaten-silver sun dropped from the sheet-metal sky, the air seemed to grow a degree colder every minute. Perhaps he had made a mistake leaving without more supplies. But he knew he had to travel light—to move slowly was to court destruction.

A single, immense snowflake the size of a leaf floated delicately down from above, swirling in a slightly off-balance circle as it dropped toward him, landing in his eye—an act of nature that made him laugh out loud, so absurd and paranoid was his sudden thought that the clouds themselves had it in for him and were tossing the flakes down like arrows one at a time, trying to hit only him. Of such conspiratorial delusions have men begun the path to madness, he thought, remembering the line from some book he had read somewhere along the line. But within a minute or two the notion seemed a lot less amusing as the sky filled with heavy flakes dropping in a vast gray sheet like a funeral shroud.

Stone had to keep spitting the flakes out as they covered his face and hair. He was so splattered with the things that he had to rub his eyes with his hands just to be able to see ahead. Not that there was much to see as the sheets of white

became waterfalls turning the very air into an impenetrable swamp. But he kept on, slogging through the freezing carpet that began to form a living field of ice beneath him.

It was when his feet began growing numb that Stone finally admitted to himself that he was in trouble. He was already tramping through several inches of the stuff as wind-blown drifts began forming walls in the forest floor around him. It was a total of over forty-five miles to the shelter. There was no way in hell he was going to make it there without stopping. He had thought the weather would hold up since it was early March, but he was wrong. It seemed that he had to learn everything the hard way. Had to have it pounded and kicked into his thick skull. Well, so be it. If he lived through it all, he was going to be the toughest motherfucker around.

After another twenty minutes, he knew he couldn't go on. His body was freezing up, the joints tightening like rust-coated gears. He could barely see anyway, as there was virtually no light coming from above, the storm clouds seeming to have dropped down to just yards above him, where they vomited out waterlogged blasts of the soggy flakes. He remembered his father telling him that as long as it still hurt, things were okay. It was when you couldn't feel your hands or your face or your feet, when it was as if there was nothing there at all that you had to worry.

Stone slowed down, trying not to panic or run in aimless, deadly circles around the snow-embalmed forest, using up all his energy and body heat. Somehow he had to find shelter, a place to weather it out. Had to find something, anything that would protect him. He edged forward like a blind man able to see only inches ahead, nearly smashing into the jutting branches of the thick pines numerous times. At last he came

to a solid rock wall set in the mountain. Reaching up with his palm, he could feel the freezing granite rock take off straight up at a ninety-degree angle. He edged along the side of the wind-smoothed face, getting down on his hands and knees and feeling along the bottom for an opening. After crawling for about fifty yards, his hand suddenly sank into the darkness.

Stone stifled his initial impulse to dive into the opening. Anything could be in there waiting—rattler, skunk. He wasn't that stupid. He congratulated himself for about half a second and then crawled away, reaching for a stick or a rock. His hand grabbed around a long, dead branch, and breaking off a four-foot piece of one of the smaller appendages, he crawled back, his jeans now sopping wet, his knees feeling like they were slabs of raw beef hanging in an icebox. He yelled out loud as he dug the twisted wooden shaft deep into the hole.

"Rats, skunks, snakes, get the fuck out. You hear me, I'm coming in here for the night." Nothing moved or squealed, so after a few seconds he rolled down inside the opening. It was a tight fit, a coffin-sized space about five feet long and two feet high, filled with leaves and small twigs that had either been blown in or used as a nest in the breeding season. He was able to squeeze inside it, but barely, and he lay still for a moment, catching his breath. It shielded him from the snow as only a few solitary flakes reached him inside. But it was still cold as ice, and the temperature was dropping all the time.

He stayed inside for just a minute, letting his heart slow down and his body temperature rise a few degrees, but as soon as he felt himself beginning to nod out into sleep, he jolted himself awake and crawled back out. Moving around

again on his hands and knees, as he still couldn't see a thing through the blizzard, Stone managed to collect an odd assortment of small rocks and twigs that he placed in a pile in front of the small crevice. He took off his jacket and rolled back inside the crack in the earth. Using a few of the thicker pieces of wood, he jammed one end of the thigh-length coat into place against the upper lip of the small overhang and then secured the other end with three rocks so that he had a canopy over him that extended out about a yard from where he lay. He reached forward, and moving very slowly, as he had to work from a contorted position, using only one arm, Stone built up a small mound of the driest of the kindling he had gathered on the dirt just outside the space. When the pile was about six inches high, he took out his lighter and flicked the striker. The damned thing didn't flame.

"Come on, come on." Stone shook it. "I took you from the supply cabinet in the bunker. You're brand-new. Don't go out on me, you son of a bitch." He struck it again and again, the lighter stubbornly resisting being lit, but at last, after nearly a dozen attempts a small cone of orange-yellow flame streamed out, flickering wildly as the winds which swept in under the canopy from the openings on each side snapped at it with cold winter lips. He rammed the lighter forward, jamming it in at the base of the kindling. Slowly, agonizingly slowly, the casings of ice melted from around the twigs, then the sap puffed out in little pops of smoke. At last the pieces caught, erupting up in streaks of flame, and within seconds the pile was ablaze. Stone quickly reached over and took more of the softball-sized rocks, building a small wall on each side of the fire so enough wind would blow through to ventilate it but not knock it out.

He fell back exhausted into the opening and allowed himself a slim smile. So far, so good. The warmth of the flames bounced back off the anchored coat, quickly permeating the hole and his body with warmth. Stone felt his joints unlocking and sensation returning to his numb hands and face as the flames burned out their life-giving energy. Within half an hour he was almost sweating from the concentrated heat and had to open one of the rock walls for more ventilation. But the damned thing worked.

Outside, the snows fell as if they were wreaking vengeance on the world, as if they wished to cover the land with an impenetrable armor of ice, of death. The waves of white descended through the night as Martin Stone half dozed, jerking awake every hour or so as the fire grew low and his body became cold, to throw more of the twigs atop it. Thus did he spend the night, in a dreamlike state where the winds and the snows and his thoughts somehow coalesced into a gauntlet down which he ran, fighting shadowy beings at every dark turn.

When he awoke, it was to the sound of a crow cawing and staring at him with a murderous intensity as it stood in the ashes of the long-dead fire. The carrion eater tilted its broad head, the feathers along its neck and shoulders rippling an iridescent black and violet, and pecked its sharp beak forward. Stone punched out awkwardly with his free arm, just missing the thing, which shot backward and up into the air screaming out in furious indignation.

"Does every goddamned creature out here want to eat me?" he yelled out from his cramped quarters, to be answered by the most perfect silence he had ever heard. Slowly he crawled forward, pushing the jacket canopy to one side so it could

be used again. But the storm was over. The ground was white as the backside of a cottontail, the sky above crystal blue, so clear one could see the craters of the daytime moon which hung lopsided in the morning sky.

He jumped up and down for a good ten minutes, trying to get blood circulating through his slowed-down system and then washed his face and drank from the soft, granular snow that lay beneath him. Once the storm season had begun, Martin knew that the skies could darken on a whim and the snows tumble for weeks without stopping. He'd have to move as fast as he could toward the bunker and not stop again until he'd reached it.

But conception was easier than implementation, for he had scarcely gone five feet when his boots cracked through the icy surface of the snow and he sank in to his knees. He pulled his legs out and began stomping forward. But it was like going through mud, through quicksand. It would take him a year to get there at this rate. He stopped in his tracks and decided to once again use his head. It pissed Stone off to do it, but he asked himself, what would Major Clayton R. Stone have done in this situation? His father, in the five years of commando-guerrilla training he had given Martin, had always stressed two things above all else: Rely only on yourself, and use what is around you. That way you'll never find yourself wanting.

He looked around, scanning the blinding snows with his hands cupped over his eyes to shield them. About fifty yards off he saw an immense tree that had apparently toppled over during the storm. It was a monster that had pulled up huge chunks of soil imbedded within its thirty-foot-long roots, which extended out from it like the dead legs of an octopus.

Not quite knowing what he would find or even what he was looking for, Stone headed over, ripping each foot straight up and forward and then down again so he didn't drag in the snow and force the freezing substance into the cuffs of his jeans.

The tree had taken a lot of the neighborhood with it— shrubs, vines, and its own huge entanglement of branches, along with three other smaller trees that happened to be in the way. It was all sort of mashed together like a dump for discarded vegetation. Stone went up to the fallen giant and scaled its side, running along the wide circumference to the base of it, which was now tilted a good thirty feet in the air. What the hell could he use? A row of branches right in a row, curved in vague bowlike shapes, caught his eye and he strode quickly down the spine of the tree, taking out his fourteen-inch blade. He chopped away at six of them and then laid them side by side in front of him. It was possible. Unlikely, ridiculous, but possible.

He jumped down from the tree, and taking some of the string laces from the pockets of his Army jacket, he laced the green, springy branches together in threes, tying the bundles at front and back. Then he placed his foot dead center of each and lashed his boots down on them. He grabbed two relatively straight poles and stood up. The whole setup looked like a ski instructor's nightmare, but he'd see. Gingerly, he placed one foot forward on the snow, supporting himself slightly with the pole—the ski stayed on the surface, only sinking in an inch or two. At least they'd work as snowshoes, he thought, placing the other leg out. It was hard maneuvering at first as each ski weighed about twenty pounds, but after a

few minutes he was moving along fairly well, even skiing along a bit from time to time.

After about ten minutes, he came to a clear slope that seemed to go down at a moderately steep angle for nearly a mile. Stone stood at the edge of the snowfield below him and looked down the side of the mountain whose bottom he couldn't even see. He gulped. He'd skied a lot as a teenager, but not for years. And these hardly looked like the pair to start practicing on. But he had no choice. Speed was his only chance. He'd done okay so far—but he'd been lucky. Stone had no illusions but that if the weather turned really foul and ugly and stayed that way for days he was finished. He'd have to take chances at every step of the way.

He looked up at the sky as if hoping to catch God's compassionate eye, mentally crossed himself, and pushed off down the side. He moved slowly at first as the lashed skis were dragging, but as he understood the proper balance and leaned back a little, the tips lifted up and he suddenly shot forward.

"Shiiit," Stone screamed out, his eyes wide with a mix of fear and excitement as he fairly flew down the slope. But he was quick, and it all came back to him instinctively as he began shifting his weight subtly from side to side, steering himself past groves of trees and the slicing boulders that popped into view every few seconds. The ride seemed to go on forever as he dodged and weaved all over the mountainside, but finally the slope grew almost flat. Then he came to the edge of a long strip of flatland that he realized was the interstate, now covered with six feet of iced-over snow. He walked over to it and then up the steep embankment, stepping sideways with the homemade skis.

Stone stood in the center of the mirror-flat ice strip that coated the highway, as if a second road had been laid and frozen during the night, and looked around trying to get his bearings. Suddenly it all came together like a jigsaw snapping into instant familiarity—Morgan's Pass with its distinctive double hump was to the right, and the stark, spearing shaft of Snowland Peak stood to the left. He was eight miles from their turnoff, and then fifteen more to the bunker. He moved quickly forward, remembering the cross-country stride he had been shown once. Within minutes he had fallen into its smooth, long motion, legs and arms all moving together in near-perfect synchronization.

He tore down the snow lane through the afternoon and had almost reached the cutoff, sighting the huge double pines that demarcated its beginning about a half mile ahead when he heard the sudden whine of motors. He stopped short, focusing his ears on the sound. What the hell was it? Cars couldn't get through this mess, and he hadn't heard or seen a plane for days. Maybe they didn't even exist anymore.

As the sounds grew louder, Stone took out his knife and started toward the embankment to the right. But he didn't make it. Lights cut through the grayness and caught him in midstride, lit by the brilliant beams. Stone stopped in his tracks, throwing a hand over his eyes as the lights were blinding. He kept his other hand gripped firmly around the handle of the hunting blade, slipping it behind his back. The snowmobiles pulled up and then grew suddenly silent as the motors were shut off.

"Well, what have we here?" a voice barked out with crude, harsh laughter. Stone stepped into the shadow between the two lights so he could see them. And he didn't like them:

two big mountain boys, their faces with that dumb, inbred look that bespoke warped chromosomes, deficient brains— and in their hands .30-30 pumps aimed straight at him. He had seen their kind here and there through the years, in small backwater towns, slinking off into shacks, never really showing their faces. They lived off their hunting and the few trinkets—bones, horns—their more presentable kin could sell in gift shops along quaint country roads where the tourists came looking for bargains. This pair looked as if they should have been thrown out with the wash—with huge, fat bodies that angled down to narrow shoulders and even smaller heads on top. They were albinos, with chalk-white skin the flat texture of the recently dead. And in the center of those pork faces were nothing but watery pink dots, eyes that couldn't stand the light of day but came out only when the sun had slunk away.

"Howdy, neighbor," Stone said cheerfully, hoping for the best, expecting the worst.

"Hey, that's a good one," the uglier of the two, a huge goiter hanging from his throat as big as an apple, laughed. "Yeah, I guess we neighbors all right." He looked over at his compatriot and winked, and the two laughed again in gales of coarse snortings. The ugly one stopped laughing. "What you got on you, boy? Maybe you be okay if you got something nice for us."

The other one, the right side of his nose eaten away from infection so the mucus flowed out the hole in a constant stream, butted in impatiently, "Ammo, you got any ammo? We need bullets, any caliber."

The uglier one's face seemed to twist up in wrinkles as his eyes grew hazy and mad. "I ain't killed for a long time.

Been such a long, long time," he said almost wistfully, as if talking of a long-lost love, and the side of his mouth became flecked with spittle and foam. He began walking toward Stone, pulling out his skinning blade and slicing it in the air.

"Should I cut his face, should I cut his throat, should I cut his heart, should I cut his scalp—"

He sang the words as if they were the psychotic's national anthem and came straight toward Stone with the look a butcher has for the squealing pig in front of him. Only, Martin Stone wasn't squealing. He stared at the obese creature, waiting until the last second when he saw the rat eyes flicker and the knife hand lunge forward. But Stone was faster. He slid to the side with a push of his skis and caught the man's arm at the wrist as it flew by. Stone slammed into the other's elbow with the blade edge of his knife, slicing right through the tendons, separating the forearm from the top in a single slash. Stone threw the bleeding appendage to the snow and, pulling his knife hand back, swung it around and forward, straight into the heart of the attacker. The man stood up straight, as if he had a poker up his ass, gasped one squeaking intake of air, and then toppled over, a geyser from his severed heart spewing out in a flood of red.

Stone turned on a dime and slid toward the second man in long, flowing strides on the skis. The noseless man watched frozen as he saw his cousin, the one who had told him what to do for the last fifteen years, get turned into a bloody carcass twitching in the snow. Stone came forward in a crouch, bending down like a speed skier as the frantic albino swung his Winchester around, trying to get a bead on him. The rifle barked twice, both bullets digging into the ice alongside Stone. He reached the snowmobile and came up suddenly, like a

striking shark rising from the depths, and sliced his arm out as far as it would go, snapping it like a whip. The razor-sharp edge cut into the attacker's throat as if it were going through butter. It ripped through the muscle, the larynx, and then the windpipe, cutting them with the perfect straight line of a surgeon.

The knife came out the other side, and Stone pulled his hand back, stepping away, as he didn't want to soil himself with the results. The albino's face had the most bizarre array of expressions fly across it in the space of a few seconds, as if he wasn't quite sure how to feel about the event. But whatever he was thinking of saying was preceded by a violent vomit of blood that exploded from the narrow white lips. Then the head, held by only the skin at the back and side, toppled slowly over from the body and spiraled down the huge stomach like a bowling ball made of blood, trailing a mass of spitting veins and tendrils. The body, as if suddenly realizing it didn't exist anymore, followed a second later, the headless stump of the neck landing only inches from the brain-oozing skull, as if it had hopes of somehow rejoining it.

CHAPTER ELEVEN

Stone pulled the bodies to the side of the road and kicked them down a long snowy slope. They moved slowly at first but then picked up speed and began tearing like toboggans, leaving a scarlet trail down the hill. He pushed one of the snowmobiles to the edge and gave it a mighty heave, and it too soared down the decline, crashing into a tree at the bottom and then sinking down into a drift. They would soon be buried by snow. No one would ever know what had occurred. Don't make trails, his father had told him. Whatever you do, wherever you go—appear and disappear like a ghost, without leaving a trace of your existence.

He mounted the remaining snowmobile and turned the key. The big machine coughed into life, vibrating fiercely beneath him. He eased back the throttle, and the thing jerked forward on the icy surface like a racehorse leaving the wire. He left the headlamp off so as not to be seen. There could be more

of them out there, and with his luck, these had been the nice ones.

"Thanks for the ride," Stone muttered, glancing down at the corpses, whose shapes he could dimly make out at the bottom of the hill as the heavy-duty Snow Tracker flew over the surface at thirty miles per hour. He had never killed before. These were his first.

I suppose I should congratulate myself, he thought with disgust, spitting a huge gob of distaste which froze in the air and flew past him like a hailstone. But all in all, this wasn't what he had in mind. He laughed aloud cynically, his lips chapping from the frigid air which swept over his face as the snow machine moved as straight and firm as a car down the highway of ice. Yeah, well, no one in this new world has anything they expect happen to them and it's tough shit, that's all. For them and me and everyone who's still alive in whatever sewer America has turned into.

And yet, it hadn't been hard at all to kill. Perhaps it was as the shaman had said—that he had the gift for it. He sure as hell didn't feel guilty. He would do it again, and again. Major Clayton R. Stone, the bastard, had taught him well. Any man who tried to kill him he would kill first. There— it was simple. A philosophy of life without a lot of complications. The rest, the ones who didn't bother him he would leave alone. But to those who wanted to play rough, he would deal out smoking spades.

He made good time and reached the cutoff within an hour. Without stopping, he wheeled the whining mechanism up and through a patch of low brush covering the start of the road. Good—it looked as if no one had been through here. What little road there was was overgrown with brambles and weeds.

It appeared more of a deer trail than anything man had ever made or used. He had to slow down as the brush grew thicker and the moon disappeared behind the thick branches of the trees above him so that he was traveling at some points in almost total darkness. But at last he made the final turn in the road, and there it was—the bunker, in all its dead glory.

Martin had lost the radio transmitter that opened the solid rock wall of the hidden shelter when the Guardians of Hell had attacked him. They wouldn't know what to do with it—unless his sister told them. She wouldn't. Stone knew that. In her own stubborn way April was one brave girl. His father fortunately had left an emergency one hidden beneath a boulder off to one side of the entrance. The rock weighed nearly three hundred pounds—to make sure that neither animal nor human was ever tempted to move it. Martin pressed his hip against the oval rock and, shifting with his entire body, managed to slide the thing aside. The transmitter was there in a plastic case to protect it from moisture and mildew. He took it out, walked over to just in front of the seemingly impenetrable rock face, and pushed the "open" button. And breathed a sigh of relief, for the moss-covered rock parted as cleanly as if split by a diamond cutter's chisel and, humming softly, slid into shafts on either side.

It felt strange to walk inside. It was all different now. His father and mother dead. His sister—God only knew. He felt their spirits all around him. The ghosts of the past shimmered through the shadows of the dimly lit outer garage like bats made of dark, ethereal matter.

"Come on, come on," Martin snapped out loud to pull himself from his black thoughts. His whole face suddenly twitched as if a jolt of current had run through him as the

door mechanism clicked loudly behind him and the four-foot-thick solid-rock doors slid automatically closed, timed to do so after eight seconds unless the "open" key was hit a second time. "Christ, I'm jittery," he mumbled to himself. "I need food, a hot shower. I'll be all right. I'll be all right." He said the words calmly, trying to smile, trying to believe he would in fact be all right. Murderers, Indians, albinos—he could take it all. It was his own heart that threatened him, the loss of the only people he had on this earth. Loneliness. He knew he couldn't go skating on that ice for long. It was thin, and the drop was a long, long way down.

The lights flicked on automatically as he opened the door to the inner chambers. There were electric eyes mounted on all the door frames so that lights were actually activated only when someone was passing through or present in a room. Another one of his father's clever energy-saving devices. The place looked just as when they'd left it just two weeks ago—suitcases half packed, clothes lying on the couches in the living room. They had only been planning to go for a few days. The auto temp controls seemed to have worked perfectly in the absence of human adjustment over the last fourteen days. Clayton had said the place could continue to warm itself, cleanse the air, even water the plants inside automatically for ten, perhaps twenty years completely on its own. Martin doubted it. But chances were he wasn't going to be around in twenty years to find out.

He hit the shower, the water instantly steaming hot from the solar heating panels camouflaged in the features of the mountain which rose above the excavated shelter. The hot water seemed to wash him clean of not just the dirt on his flesh, but inside too, so that when he emerged his body

actually felt lighter, as if a load of emotional baggage had been taken off his shoulders and swept down the drain into the underground stream below.

He walked through the house wearing just a towel around his waist, dripping a small trail of water on the floors and carpets he passed over—something his mother had scolded him for countless times. Well, it was his place now—for better or worse. He would do as he pleased. Martin made his way to his room and took down a set of still-detergent-scented clothes—a pair of black jeans and black sweat shirt. He was tired as hell, his legs aching everywhere, charley-horsed from the hours of skiing. But there was something he had to do. Something he'd waited years to do.

His father had had a special room that no one had been permitted to enter. The Major had spent hours, days sometimes, in there. He would always explain it all by saying he was conducting experiments to make more devices for the shelter. Martin hadn't felt able to go in it right after his father's death. His domineering presence had still been too strong. But now . . .

He walked up to the black steel door that stood at the deepest portion of the bunker and waved his hand in front of the glowing amber electric eye that guarded it like some photon dragon. The door didn't budge. So Major Clayton was having his fun. Even after his body was gone, his mind wanted to live, playing tricks on those whose blood still ran hot. But Stone had his own tricks. He had watched once, years before, hidden behind some crates as his father had entered the room. What the hell had he done? He closed his eyes and searched for the memory, trying to bring it into clearer focus. He saw his father's hand going back and forth

in front of the eye, waving out a precoded signal that the thing was programmed to accept. Yes, three—and—two— then five. Something like that. He tried ten combinations before he found the right one and the solid slab of steel slid open with a whisper on ball-bearing runners.

Stone whistled out loud. It looked like Frankenstein's laboratory inside, with a vast array of incomprehensible devices lining every square inch of the place. Off to one side stood what was clearly a large radio transmitter and receiver from which Stone could dimly hear someone calling out a CB code. So his father had lied about that too. He had always told them that the high levels of radiation and magnetism in the atmosphere had made any reception impossible. Again Stone felt a discomforting sensation of rage toward the old man who had played games with them for five goddamned years. Had lied at every step of the way. Had played with them like puppets on his paternalistic strings.

He walked across the twenty-five-by-sixty-foot space glancing around everywhere at the flashing lights, the video display monitors flickering out sine curves and parabolas made of wavy orange light. At the far end of the room stood what was clearly the lab's main computer, a bulky affair with keyboard and screen atop a Formica table and three immense steel boxes piled one atop the other that rose behind it. With the kind of miniaturization that his father had been playing around with, the combined power of that much memory must make this a super-computer. In his room in the shelter, Martin had had his own Macintosh, with which he had written, played video games, and done drawing and animation. The whole family had used their own personal models—if nothing

else, to give them something to do so they wouldn't go mad from the boredom.

He flicked the "on" switch to the monster machine and then depressed the ENTER key just to see what would happen. The thing chugged a few times as electrons flowed through it, bringing it awake, and then green words scrolled up onto the screen. Stone stared in disbelief at the message from the grave.

CHAPTER
TWELVE

"If you're reading this, it most likely means that I'm already dead. It also means that you've found out that the world outside is not as I told you. This will doubtless just add fuel to your fire of thinking me a manipulative, tyrannical old man who couldn't bear the idea of people deciding things for themselves. And who knows—there's probably some truth in it. But that's not why, in my own heart, I did it. At first I thought of telling you all that the bombs hadn't destroyed everything, but when I listened over the shortwave in the months afterward I heard a radio chronology of the breakdown of a civilization as people described the savagery that was erupting all around them. I heard the screams come over the air as people were hacked to death while begging for help over their transmitters. Sometimes the screams hurt my eardrums, they were so loud. And so I decided for better or worse to keep us all in here until things had worked their

way out—until the worst of the beasts had destroyed one another. And I would do it again. There's life out there, Martin, but none of it worth meeting.

"When the nuke war started, though each side launched tremendous quantities of missiles, only a dozen or so actually got in. There was one thing all the theoreticians hadn't counted on—the EMPs. Electromagnetic pulses put out by the first wave filled the atmosphere with so much electric garbage—created such a shield of interference—that the rest either detonated high in the stratosphere or fell harmlessly into oceans and forests. But all communications equipment—TV, radio, phones, and much of the power supply of both America and Russia—was knocked out.

"Then the European Military Coalition and the Third World Alliance stepped in—they'd had enough. And who could blame them? Between us, America and Russia had come close to adding another dead planet to the solar system—just what it needed. Using only conventional weapons, the EMC and the TWA invaded in an armada of ships and planes that made D-Day look like an excursion. And when it was all over, virtually all of both superpowers' military capabilities and remaining nukes had been destroyed. Never again would either nation be able to threaten the world. The Euro armies withdrew, leaving the U.S. in a state of virtual quarantine, with land mines, nets, and battleships surrounding her on every side so that she could not wreak her murderous nature on the rest of mankind. The same was done to the Soviets.

"After that, it was downhill in a wagon for us over here. There were countless mutinies, uprisings in what remained of the military and the CIA. Everyone wanted to rule—and so none of them did. The President and Congress were finally

forced to flee the capital as angry mobs of tens of thousands stormed the place, demanding food, medicine, uncontaminated water. None of them has been heard from since. That was over four years ago.

"With my radio equipment I was able to get a general picture of what was evolving. At the very beginning it wasn't so bad. People tried to cope, tried to remain human to one another. But as the remaining stocks of food and fuel grew scarce, people began turning on one another, fighting like dogs over scraps. Things began being decided by guns and knives. And as always happens as society reverts to barbarism, the meanest, the cruelest, those who could kill and intimidate better than the rest rose to the top. Within one year America had deteriorated into a dark age not unlike the early middle ages. Plagues, pestilences as murderous as anything mentioned in the Bible hit the U.S., and each city, each little town became its own walled-off society, superstitious, afraid, and extremely violent toward anyone who came and tried to take what little was theirs.

"I kept hoping it would get better, Martin. Prayed that it would. I vowed that as soon as the reports I heard over the radio grew even a little brighter—as soon as I heard that there were at least pockets of humanity trying to rise—we would leave this place. But those words never came. Instead, there were only pleadings for help, people begging for someone to come and save them from the warlords, the murderers, the cannibals that were upon them. Then even the radio transmissions grew less and less until there were only a few.

"Things are bad out there. From some of the transmissions I heard, bad beyond belief, bad even beyond the living hells I experienced in my years as a Ranger and in Special Forces.

I'm sorry, Martin. Sorry that I had to do it all the way I did, sorry that you and I never communicated the way I had always hoped we would, that we somehow always disappointed one another. Sorry for the whole rotten world you and your sister were born into. At any rate, I can only assume that you will be going out there. And were I you, I would do the same. Be wary, Martin. I've shown you much in the ways of destruction. You'll need every bit of this knowledge. I wish I could have taught you more, but as you remember, there was great resistance from you at certain times.

"I've spent much of these last years when I was holed up in here putting down everything I know on computer. If you need it, it's here. Every bit of data I possess on warfare, fighting, siege, espionage, and every other goddamned thing a man could want to know on how to kill another man is in here. In this computer. Should you ever want to use it, just type in 'Directory' and 'Enter.' The subjects are broken down alphabetically from A to Z.

"This probably all sounds pretty bizarre to you—and doubtless confirms your belief that your old man went over the edge at the end. But I just want to end this computerized postmortem with a final thought, and then if you don't want to you'll never have to hear from me again for the rest of your life.

"You never asked me why I was a soldier for all those years, and I never volunteered the information. But I'll tell you now. It sounds corny, Martin, but it was to defend freedom. And particularly the freedom of the little guy not to be stepped on by the bastards of this world. I made a lot of mistakes along the way, as did my country—but for me it was something I had to do. A man ultimately is alone, Martin,

completely alone. Whoever you share your life with, may they be inches away, still we are born alone, live that way, and sink back into the ground on our own. And what you do must be decided by you, and only you. The kind of person you want to be. The side you choose in the ongoing struggle of good and evil that man carries with him through history like a cancerous growth on his soul. And the odd thing is, no one really cares what you think or do. Only yourself. But you know. You know deep inside, and every action defines you in terms of the light or the darkness. Every action makes you more of a man or—something else. Something without a heart, a soul. Something that preys on its fellowman like wolves on a carcass.

"I was a Ranger, Martin. That was my self-definition: to liberate the oppressed. I taught you what I knew so that you might carry on the battle and carry the flame. That you might be the Last Ranger, the last son of a bitch dumb enough to care what happens to those around you. It's your choice, son. God be with you. And know that whatever you think of me— in my heart I always loved you and did what I thought was right."

The computer speech ended, and the screen scrolled up to the directory as Martin Stone stared up at the monitor, his jaw hanging half open. He didn't know anymore if the old man was crazy, if he himself was crazy, if the whole world was crazy. The word hardly had meaning anymore. His brain tried to digest the information as he turned the screen off and walked from the room, but it just made him tired. It was too much on top of everything else he had just been through. He walked wearily to his room and into bed. He was asleep in minutes. And in his dreams he saw April being tortured, raped

by the two albinos he had killed. But as he came running toward her, it was as if he could only move in slow motion, and no matter how much his legs pumped he never got any closer to her. From out of the sides of the dream came men running at him, every weapon imaginable in their hands, slashing, firing at him while far above him his father flew in wide circles with eyes of glowing green digital numbers.

When he awoke, Martin dressed in a flash and headed for the weapons room. It was time to go. Time to begin using whatever he had inside him and find his sister before it was too late. He went around the shelves of the large room, which were filled with a warehouse worth of modern murder wares. Rifles of every caliber, automatic weapons, ground-to-air missile launchers lined the walls and shelves of the concrete-walled room as if it were a munitions dump. His father had planned well—Martin had to give him that. There were enough weapons here to stock an army. The only problem was ammunition. The main shipment had been scheduled to arrive the day after the H-bombs landed. Needless to say, it never came. Still, there was enough for the moment. That was for damned sure.

He had trained in the use of everything from a snub-nosed .38 to a tripod-mounted 50mm and every other weapon that could blow a man to hell and back. They had had constant firing practice on the range at the rear of the bunker, really just a cave that went nowhere. Over the years father and son had blasted deep into the cold rock, widening it by yards, extending it backward nearly ten feet. Martin had grown fond of certain tools of the trade, finding them particularly suited to his hands, his eyes, giving him that extra sureness of grip, that millisecond of added speed that could mean life or death

in the wastelands outside. He had been a fool the first trip out, taking only a 12-gauge shotgun. He would not make the same mistake twice.

He reached up and took down the black leather holster containing his huge Ruger Redhawk .44 magnum. Thirteen and a half inches long, the six-round, stainless-steel pistol with rubber Pachmayer grips was a monster—but it could stop one too. And with its integral base system—barrel recessed to accept scope mount—fitted with Leupold 5X scope with floating red sight dot, the .44 was accurate to one hundred yards—powerful stuff for a handgun. He strapped the quick-draw holster onto his right hip and then took down the Uzi 9mm autopistol which, with its thirty-shot clip or fifty-shot banana load, gave Stone plenty of fast takeout firepower. He put it in a shoulder holster on the left side of his chest, the magazine right next to it for instant snap-in. His father had told him so many war stories about how he'd saved his ass with a hidden gun that Stone also took a five-shot S&W .38— a Bodyguard Airweight with two-inch barrel and stripped-down plastic body. The pistol was so light and slim that he was able to slip it in a clip holster just inside his right boot.

He walked on to the back shelves containing the heavier stuff, and after a few minutes of deliberation took down a Browning BPS sawed-off 12-gauge shotgun which could take five rifled rounds. Just in case he needed some long-range firepower, Stone went up on the sliding ladder to a top shelf and took down a Barnett Model 82 .50-cal sniper rifle. With its Aimsight 10X infrared scope and three-thousand-yard firing capability with accuracy, the twelve-round magazine rifle could strike like the hand of God far out of sight of its target.

He carried the weapons in his arms through the house and

out to the front entrance chamber where the vehicles—two cars and a motorcycle—stood covered in plastic tarps, well oiled and ready to go. The cars would be impossible, but the bike . . . With the special wide-tread, grooved snows, it could cut over even fully iced terrain. His father had had some special racks mounted on the back of the Harley 1200 Electro-glide so it could carry much bigger loads than usual. With side bolts and ball-bearing swivels, the thing could be mounted into a mini-battlewagon. Stone stacked the bigger weapons in expandable sealed cases in the back of the bike, distributing the weight evenly on each side. The Harley already had a .50-caliber machine gun mounted dead center of the front fender, with autoclip loading capacity from a belt that ran alongside.

"Do not go gentle into that good night," Martin muttered to himself as he stared down at the wide double-seat bike. It looked mean and fast, like some reptilian thing with tongue ready to spit murderous fire, but he'd need even more. He walked quickly back to the weapons room and took down the Luchaire 89mm Rocket Launcher LRAC and a case containing ten rockets. It was hand-held, and one of its projectiles could take out a tank—even a chopper. Back in the outer chamber Stone mounted the 89mm bazooka-shaped device onto a set of the heavy-duty brackets that enabled it to swing out in any direction or be locked tight against the side facing at a slightly upward angle and to the rear. The ammo feeder containing the ten shells he attached just below the launching tube. He'd have to pop out one of the rockets and manually push it into the firing chamber. Still, it could be fired and reloaded within ten seconds. It would do. He loaded up the bike with supplies—water, concentrated food, a down sleep-

ing bag and mini-tent, and every other goddamned thing he could stuff into the plethora of watertight boxes that straddled the whole back end of the motorcycle.

He had everything now—except a coherent plan. What exactly was he going to do once he got into Denver and found himself surrounded by ten thousand leather-jacketed bikers looking for blood? Grudgingly, feeling like an idiot, Stone walked back to his father's lab and the computer that the Major had sent him a condensed history of the world over. Well, if he'd spent five years spilling his guts into this thing, Martin thought, he might as well take a look and see what it had to offer. He turned it on and called up the central directory, where a vast array of choices all placed alphabetically ran in columns down the screen. He searched until he found ONE MAN AGAINST LARGE STATIC FORCE, and pressed the three-digit number next to it. Instantly, the screen filled with pages of information which quickly rolled by him: how to survey the terrain, how to estimate numbers of men, amounts of weapons. How to set up traps, cut communications, place bombs. How, in other words, to disrupt an entire city and bring it to its knees.

Stone sat in front of the screen for nearly an hour, going over the fifty pages of green-lit words twice before he was satisfied that he understood even half of it. But the Major had given him a lot of ideas. And a lot of options. He turned the computer off and headed out, closing the door almost sacredly behind him. It was weird to have such a source of information. It was as if his father wasn't really dead, and he was reminded of his peyote hallucination. He shuddered at the memory and headed down the hall, checking the central panel of the computer that controlled the shelter's living func-

tions. All was still working perfectly. He didn't have to make a single adjustment.

Feeling ready to take on a whole goddamned army, he opened the huge stone doors with the transmitter and twisted the throttle of the Electroglide 1200 so it edged slowly out into the weeds. He got off the bike as the doors closed firmly behind him, wondering if he'd ever see this place again. Then he moved the boulder and reburied the transmitter underground, where it would be for April should she make her way back on her own.

Feeling as if he were burying his past beneath the boulder, Stone got on the big bike and without another glance backward shot forward down the weed-covered road as the sun twinkled through the branches in a jerky, broken rhythm. He reached the interstate in just over half an hour and headed up onto it. Some of the surface snow had melted a bit, but now that the direct rays of the sun were past, it was re-forming into ice atop half-frozen snow. The wheels, a good four inches wider than the normal cycle tire, easily dug into the substance, and once he felt comfortable on the treacherous surface Stone had the bike up to fifty without skidding or shimmying an inch.

After he had gone about ten miles—near, he figured, where the Guardians had attacked them—Stone looked around for the Winnebago, but he couldn't find a trace. Whatever had been left of it had no doubt been stripped of every square inch of its usable materials, and the rest lay buried under the early snows. There wasn't a hell of a lot to go around anymore—people seemed to use every bit down to the bone. He saw other wrecked cars, the blackened shells of them anyway. They were old, though, probably destroyed within months of

the war. Even the metal skeletons had become so corroded and pitted that they looked as if they would fall apart at a touch. He saw skeletons of people too—and animals. Every mile or so something that had died or been killed flashed by the bike.

"A laugh a minute here in 1995," Stone yelled out into the wind as he saw a whole family of riddled skeletons sitting in the few pieces that were left of an ancient station wagon. "On the way to the mall—and whammo, huh?" he yelled out to them as he rode by. Then he shook his head in disbelief. Christ, he was going half crazy himself. He'd better watch who he talked to. The dead weren't very conversational.

But when he had gone another thirty or so miles down the snow-blanketed highway, he found living souls who seemed quite interested in him. They had a roadblock erected of wooden planks on sawhorses, and five men stood in front with rifles, old and coated with dirt, in their hands. Stone slowed the bike, edging his finger along the left handle toward the trigger of the front-mounted .50-caliber machine gun.

"Just slow down there, fellow," one of the men, wearing a porkpie, screamed, holding his double-barreled shotgun a little higher. "You ain't going nowhere till you talk to us."

"What do you want to talk about?" Stone asked.

"Talk about where you're heading and what you're carrying in the back of that there contraption. Christ, he got a shitload of stuff up there, ain't he, boys." The rednecked face laughed, pointing to the back of the bike, which was piled high with black ominous-looking boxes.

"Sorry, fellas," Stone said, keeping his eyes fixed on every one of them, waiting for the slightest motion to pull the

trigger. "This stuff's already consigned to somebody else by order of the highest authority."

"And what authority is that?" the leader of the roadblock crew asked contemptuously.

"My authority," Stone said, staring back with eyes as cold as steel on a winter night. "I'm coming through. I've got work to do. Get those roadblocks out of my way or I'm taking them out."

"Taking them out." The man laughed. "Oh, please be my guest." He swept his arm down mockingly toward Martin as if bowing. Stone tilted the bike in a flash so it was facing forward and pulled his finger hard on the trigger. The .50-caliber mounted on the front fender spat out a mouthful of slugs that tore into the wooden planks and sent them rocketing thirty feet into the air, turning end over end as they rained a blizzard of particles and sawdust down on the crowd of men. They looked stunned. Stone pulled out the Uzi 9mm from his left shoulder holster and slammed in the clip. He started the bike forward.

Most of the crowd stood there frozen, unable to deal mentally with the burst of power they had seen him send out. But there always had to be one—or two—who would try. The leader and his main man walked forward and leveled their rifles at him. Stone ducked beneath the low bulletproof visor on the front of the bike and with his right hand let loose a burst from the automatic pistol, keeping his finger on the trigger as he sprayed a two-second burst. The men jerked suddenly like robots gone haywire as red holes appeared on various parts of their anatomies. They they dropped without a sound.

Stone moved forward, his Uzi trained on the crowd. But

they'd had enough and threw their weapons down, staring with terror-stricken eyes and pasted smiles as they looked at this avenging angel who played with them like so many toys.

"No more roadblocks, okay?" Stone told them. "Everyone who wants to passes through here. No tolls, no taxes, no nothing. We're all going to start civilizing around here again." He looked down at the flopping bodies. "And on their grave markers have it written, I Died of Greed. I'll be back to check it all out. Believe me—I'll be back." He shot ahead, wheels rolling over the random pieces of wooden roadblock that lay, still smoking, on the ice highway.

CHAPTER THIRTEEN

He reached the outskirts of Denver just after nightfall. Even now, after the war, after the descent of American civilization, the city was lit up with a thousand twinkling lights of activity. But the hills around it were dark, deserted. Stone parked on an outcropping of mountain road he'd been riding and lay down at the side, looking down with the long-range infrared he'd taken from the supply room. He turned the focus and two miles off he could see them—streets, people walking. But what kind of people?

It was as if somebody's bad dream had been let out in the streets of Denver—hulking figures covered with guns, knives, and faces that shouldn't be allowed around mirrors. Many of them, whose features he could dimly make out on the streets where bare light bulbs were strung up on poles, serving as makeshift street lamps, seemed to have been in numerous fights as large chunks of their faces were missing, whole

sides of mouths, ears—even a scalp or two totally torn from the skull. Here and there, moving among them, he sighted members of the Guardians with their distinctive black leather jackets with skull-over-H-bomb that adorned their backs. Where they walked, the others stepped aside.

It was one fucking tough city. "Well, I'm starting at the top anyway," Stone said, trying to enthuse himself as he pulled the glasses up and back into their case. He remounted the bike and headed back around the side of the mountain out of view of the city where he found an unused side road. He drove for a good two miles, hearing and seeing no one, not even a flicker of flame until he found what he was looking for: a thick growth of thornbushes—about fifty of them growing together, a briar patch into which not even a jackrabbit would wish to try his luck. But Stone would have to. He parked the bike and began hacking away at the thick, junglelike growth with the huge Bo Randall custom bowie that his father had presented to him on his sixteenth birthday. It was another gift that at the time seemed inappropriate and old-fashioned. Martin remembered looking awkwardly at the old man as he had presented it to him in a box with purple velvet lining.

And now he was chopping through vines as thick as a python's neck with it, and grateful to have it in his hands. Things were changing—everything moving in such an off rhythm and nonlinear way that he could only sit back and watch it and wait for the next thing that tried to kill him. After hours of being stabbed and poked in the arms and face and having whole chunks of skin gouged out by the probing thorns, Stone created enough of a pathway that he was able to drag the motorcycle nearly twenty feet inside it to a space

he had carved out in the center. After taking what he needed from the supply boxes, he lay a plastic-aluminum camouflage tarp over the bike and set it carefully on its side. As he exited through the channel of thorns, he pulled the branches back in place, and using balls of the thorny stalks he had chopped, he blocked the path with the same seemingly impenetrable wall that had existed before. He stood several yards away and looked down on his creation. It was perfect, appearing totally untouched by human hands. Stone started down the side of the mountain toward Denver and the madness that awaited him there.

But the moment he actually reached the bottom of the mountain and stepped onto a square of sidewalk at the very abrupt edge of the town, he could see that it was even worse than he'd thought. Four poles greeted the new traveler to Denver, poles on every one of the outer corners that ringed the city. And on them hung human heads in various states of decomposition—from freshly bleeding to leathery and shrunken with hideous, wrinkled smiles on inscrutable faces. They looked down on Stone as he walked onto the main thoroughfare of the city, screaming out a tale of horror through lips that couldn't move. He mentally felt for the different holsters he wore under his bulky fatigue jacket and felt reassured at their presence. At least he'd have a fighting chance, though he prayed in the very bottom of his soul that he didn't end up like those poor bodiless beings twenty feet up with spikes slammed through their powdery brains.

Those that passed him by in the street seemed to pay Stone little attention. Many of them wore fatigues and camouflage jackets. Everyone in the town looked as if he was from some cutthroat organization or other—and all of them seemed ready

to slice the other man's throat at the drop of a hat, or an insult. Stone kept his senses fully alert, scanning everyone around him with careful eyes. In the streets more and more drunken slobs lay snoring facedown in their own vomit. Pickpockets and scavengers went through their things, taking all that they could find. Stone did nothing to stop them. It was a hard world.

As he reached the central part of the city, things got more lively. Motorcycles roared up and down Fairfax Avenue as Guardians did tricks atop them or came at each other playing chicken. Myriad small bars and strip joints lined the street, sleazy places with hookers with bags under their eyes and junkies with concave faces peering solemnly through the windows, looking for their next fix, their next john, their next anything. But Stone walked on. He wanted to go where the head honchos had their fun. A man suddenly lurched toward him, and Stone caught him by the arm, ready to smash his elbow into the face. But the guy was just drunk, his eyes all red and veined.

"Where's the action around here, pal?" Stone asked in a friendly voice as the man looked startled.

"Oh, I thought you were a ripper. They take everything, you know—rip you up sometimes too. Use razors, cut faces, they like to cut," the man babbled on, nearly incoherent.

"Where's the action?" Stone pressed him. "Where can a guy have some real fun—you know—if he has some money?" He reached in one of his side pockets, took out a dollar, and handed it to the man.

"You got a real dollar. Son, you giving me a dollar just to tell you." He laughed. "God bless you. This is my lucky day." Stone couldn't tell at first if the man was mocking him

or not. But he seemed so happy it apparently meant a dollar bill was worth a hell of a lot more than it had for a long, long time. He'd have to be more careful with money—with everything—or he'd attract attention to himself.

"Sure," the drunken man said, stepping back and pointing down the street. "You can't miss it. There's only one really big place here, Rommel's. Rommel runs it, runs everything in this town. He's the head of the Guardians here, whole state too. Just two blocks dead ahead on the right-hand side." The drunk started to walk off, somehow suddenly pathetically aware of what a mess he was as he glanced down at his fecal-messed pants and moth-eaten jacket stained with a variety of unpleasant substances. He glanced up again at Stone. "But listen, boy. You got to be a killer for them to even let you in the damned place. Those guys are some bad dudes."

"I think I can pass the door requirements," Stone said, heading back up the street. It got more and more raucous the closer he came to the brightly lit bar, with its big, flickering neon lights of women revealing their naked bodies in three stages, ending with their naked breasts and triangles all lit up in red before starting the cycle over again. Long rows of motorcycles of every size and shape, many of them adorned with spikes, chains, furs, and things that Stone didn't want to examine too closely, lined the side of the street, extending off for nearly the entire block in each direction. A large group of about a dozen men were fighting wildly in the center of the street, punching one another, kicking teeth out, throwing each other all over the place. Stone carefully made his way between them, slamming his elbow out from time to time as one of the flailing bodies grew too close, until at last he

reached the door and the Neanderthal bouncer who stood just inside.

"Where the hell do you think you're going, asshole?" a half ton of pockmark-cratered flesh asked, his face devoid of life, his eyes as narrow and cold as a drop of frozen blood.

"Going inside to see my mother," Stone smirked, his hand ready to snap out and do some quick and painful damage if the need arose.

The bear-sized bouncer looked at Stone with incredulity for about five seconds and then he laughed. Just one quick, sharp sound, then his face returned to its fixed, psychotic mask. "You t'ink you mom's in dere," the man said, apparently having some trouble with the finer points of the English language. "You fin' yo' mum in dere you say hi fo' me." Then he laughed again, just once, at his own conception of a joke.

"Yeah, I'll certainly do that," Stone said, stepping forward and past him as the bouncer moved to the side. "And I'll pay my respects to yours too," Stone added, moving on before the towering slab's pea-sized brain could send the message to the body beneath it to move. He made his way through the crowd of pungent-breathed drinkers who screamed incoherently into one another's faces, spittle dribbling down unshaven cheeks, or exchanged blows on various parts of the anatomy to see who was the better man, and various other loud and generally painful activities that was their idea of having fun.

The place was long and wide, with raw planking on the floors and walls, giving it a somewhat rustic appearance. Two long redwood bars ran down each side, atop which girls of all sizes and ages wearing little or nothing danced while

the drooling men below fondled them and threw trinkets and coins at their various charms. And below the bars, Stone saw as he grew closer, were glass aquariums set side by side all the way down the sides of the room. The tanks were filled with snakes, rats, lizards, every goddamned thing you wouldn't want to look at, each in its own four-by-five-foot enclosure. The imprisoned wildlife stared up angrily and struck out as arms above them reached past for drinks, but their claws and fangs bounced harmlessly off the thick glass tops and they fell back down, enraged.

Stone leaned over what was a case full of timber rattlers, their rattles vibrating like mad as they gave him the once-over. Stone, not letting his arms touch the glass, no matter how thick it was, leaned over and ordered a beer from the bartender, who looked at him with a distasteful squint, then coughed violently, spitting onto the floor. He gave Stone a quick once-over and then handed him a dirt-streaked glass of homemade beer. Everyone in the goddamned place looked at you like you had just ground their grandmother up into Shake 'N Bake.

"Nice place," Stone said, taking a swig of the sour, thick-tasting beverage that seemed about seventy-five percent foam. "Bunch of real swingers here." The bartender glanced over at the man trying to engage him in human conversation.

"Yeah," the barkeep grunted, not unwilling to talk, as half of those in the place couldn't put a sentence together that was going in one direction. "Yeah, these are a great bunch of guys." He smiled for a second and twitched and looked away. His face was narrow and straight like a weasel's, and his eyes were so far back in his head that it looked as if they

had fallen into a crevice and couldn't quite find their way out.

"Yeah, got everything here," he went on. "You name it, pal. Girls, drugs, corpses—anything. What's your pleasure?" He turned and stared at Stone, his face again twitching violently, whatever drugs he was on making his whole body tremble and spasm wildly just beneath the skin, as if his muscles were trying to escape. "Now we got mescaline, Methedrine, codeine, heroin, cocaine, LSD, angel dust, THC, PCP, PCB, and TLC. Got smoke from ten countries, hash from five. Got ups, downs, sideways, and everything in between. All guaranteed by the house to be fresh and made by guys who took more than kindergarten in organic chemistry. What gets you straight?" The barkeep stopped talking, though his white lips continued to quiver like little worms on the end of a precipice.

Stone glanced down as he saw a rattler suddenly shoot up from its coiled position in a corner of a glass case and slam into the glass just below him. The long fangs of the serpent cracked into the partition as it struck like a blur over and over—its jaws, its wide, dark mouth reaching for him. Dark brown venom squirted out and streaked the underside of the glass. Then the thing fell back into the sand on the bottom, where it raced around wildly, maddened that it couldn't reach what it wanted to kill.

"Actually, I was looking for a girl," Stone said, taking another mouthful of the home brew, which at least was warming his stomach as he looked back up at the bartender.

"Oh, a girl," the man said, disappointed as he washed a glass with a filthy rag and put it up on a shelf. "There's enough of them around here to service an army. Lots of 'em

upstairs. All over the place. You pays five dollars for the ugly ones, ten for the foxes, and twenty for the virgins—or what passes for virgin around here. You gets thirty minutes—there's rooms upstairs. They cost another five dollars—you got?"

"Very reasonable rates," Stone muttered, "but actually I was looking for a particular girl."

"There are no particular girls, fellow," the keep snapped impatiently. "Just girls. What the hell do you want anyway? They all got the same things, right?" Suddenly they heard screams and turned to see two men fighting. One of them pulled out an ice pick and in a flash stabbed it into the other's heart—all the way in. Then he stepped back. The dead man looked down at his chest, then up at his attacker, then down again. Then he fell with a look of acute surprise on his blood-draining face. The killer turned, slid the pick up a long sleeve, and disappeared into the crowd. Within twenty seconds at most, two men came over and lifted the corpse, carrying it out of a swinging door into a room in back.

"So how many of those do you have a night?" Stone asked, finishing his beer and turning back to the bar.

"Oh, a good night, five, six. Been getting a little slow lately. You know how it is. But this is where they all come to die. They think they're going to do the killing, but that's not how it ends up. No, sir. This place is a regular disposal center for the scum of the earth. Why, we do the whole world a favor with our service."

There was the sound of raucous laughter from a table, and Stone glanced over to see ten or so of the Guardians, their black leather jackets draped over wide, steamroller shoulders, drinking and rolling dice. Women were all over them like

cats, sitting on laps or on the floor at their feet, stroking their thick legs. A drunk stumbled too close to one of them and crashed into the back of his chair, making the dice the gang member held in his hand pop up and come down craps. He rose, his face beet-red beneath his black beard, and turned to the man.

"You made me miss my throw, asshole, so I'm going to have to throw you." He reached down with massive arms and picked the struggling fool straight up in the air, holding him with both arms high above his head. The offending party screamed a drunken howl as he stared down from eight feet above the floor as the Guardians screamed with laughter, pounding their fists so hard on the table that half the bottles and glasses on it tumbled down, smashing on the hard wood planking below.

"Heads or tails?" the huge bearded gang member screamed out, setting his legs for the throw. "I'll bet you a hundred bucks—that's American dollars—it's heads."

"You're on," one of the gang, nearly as big as the thrower, yelled back, standing up and ripping a wad of bills from one of the greasy pockets of his half-torn leather jacket and throwing the money down in the middle of the table. The thrower took a deep breath, let his thigh-sized arms down just a little, and then heaved up and out with all his might in an explosive effort. The drunk soared in a high trajectory, a blurred mass of legs and arms. He flew almost fifteen feet as the masses leaped out of the way, and then came down on his head so hard that the skull cracked right across the top like an egg and opened up as if the invisible hand of God were about to

pop it into a frying pan. The drunk's brain slurped out in a big wet lump and slid across the floor, undulating between the legs of the drinkers at the bar like some kind of sea slug searching for a cave.

CHAPTER FOURTEEN

Then everything happened real fast. Stone heard a scream, a girl's scream, shrill and piercing. He turned his head to the table filled with the bikers and saw one of them at the back smashing a girl's head down onto the side of a chair again and again. Her head came bobbing up into view for just a second, and Martin's heart skipped ten beats. It was April. He tore forward like a rocket, knocking several of the partygoers off their feet, shot around the side of the table, and grabbed the man's right hand, which was holding the blonde head. He whipped the biker's arm up and around before the man realized what was happening and then slammed the heel of his hand in just under the chin. The three-hundred-pound-plus hulk of a thing flew backward as if he'd been struck by a cannon and crashed onto a table behind him, breaking its legs, sending it in pieces to the floor. Stone reached down for the girl, her face bleeding and cut open in numerous

places. He looked closely into her eyes. It wasn't April. It might have been her sister—but it wasn't her. Shit! He'd done it now. But there was no pulling back. He'd have to play it to the hilt.

"Mister, you are about to die," the biker he had struck said slowly, enunciating each word. The others watched as they burped and drank and slobbered over the girls sitting next to them. A good fight was always a pleasure to see.

"Didn't mean to hit you so hard," Stone said as he pushed the wounded girl away, who scrambled off through the crowd on her hands and knees. "Thought she was a piece I was looking for. Little bitch ran out on me—after I'd paid a hundred dollars for her."

"*You* didn't mean to hit *me* so hard," the biker sneered as he came forward, raising crushing fists. "Asshole, that was the best—and last—shot you'll ever get in your life. I wasn't looking. Now I'm looking." He leaped toward Stone with a pulverizing left hook that could have dented in the side of a car. Only Stone wasn't a car. He slipped inside the huge arms and slammed his right elbow into the ganger's throat. The man stopped as if shot and gasped for air, his eyeballs looking as if they were about to explode out as he stumbled around in a little circle an inch at a time, pirouetting on the tips of his toes.

Stone turned toward the Guardians, who were a little quieter now, the smiles gone from their faces. They stared at him as if they were glaciers ready to crush him into paste. "Like I say," Stone went on evenly, meeting them all eye to eye, "it was an honest mistake. Thought she was mine."

"Well now, you're just going to have to pay for that mistake, ain't you," Rommel snarled from the table. "'Cause I

don't think Cut here is going to be able to handle your apologies. He's not the most diplomatic kind." The others laughed again and slammed the table with their drinking mugs.

"Come on, Cut, get him, get the little bastard," they cheered their boy on, certain that Stone had gotten in a few lucky shots but that in the long run—that being another ten or twenty seconds—he would just be something to be cleaned off the floor and put in the body wagon out back.

The stricken biker at last was able to suck in air. He glared at Stone with a look of purest hate and slowly pulled a long, pearl-handled blade from his side. "I'm gonna carve you up, little pig. I'm going to hear you squeal." He came toward Stone crouching down, waving his knife hand forward. He was one of the best with a blade. He sighted up the stranger's stomach. He'd cut him there first, watch the guts fall out. Then he'd slice his throat.

"I should warn you that I'm going to kill you," Stone said with a look of sincere concern as he waited, his arms crossed in front of him. His father had always told him to never underestimate the power of getting your opponent angry, making him lose himself in his emotions, even for a fraction of a second.

"You're going to kill me, you little fucking twerp," the biker screamed out, humiliated in front of all his fellows. He shot forward, stabbing out with the knife with surprising speed. Stone stepped sharply to the side, sliding outside the enraged bull of a man, and then stepped in again. He wrapped his arm around the man's neck from behind and with a blur of motion dropped down to one knee, pulling the biker's legs right out from under him. The huge body came crashing down onto the upright knee just below the base of the neck with

the power of a sledgehammer going sixty miles an hour. There was a loud crack that could be heard around the entire bar as the spinal cord snapped in two like a chicken bone pulled apart at Sunday dinner.

Stone pulled his knee away and stood up, letting the body slide down onto the floor. The biker's eyes were still wide open, looking straight up at the ceiling, but he wasn't seeing too much as the cells within his eyes already began starting to cool on the quick road to disintegration. From living to dead in three seconds.

Stone turned and looked at the table of bikers, waiting for whoever to make a move. He hadn't wanted it to happen quite like this—but he'd take out most of them before he was gone. There would be some satisfaction in that. The bikers looked edgily at one another and started to rise, but Rommel threw his hands in the air, warding them back.

"Hold on a minute, boys. This guy's got balls—balls bigger than my fucking feet—to walk in here, come up to our table, and kill one of my men. I like you, asshole. Come sit down." He slammed his huge leather-gloved hand down on the chair next to him and stared off his own men, who didn't seem to like the idea at all.

"Where the hell'd a guy like you learn tricks like that?" Rommel asked him, stroking his wiry bramble bush of a beard. "I mean no offense, you ain't no wimp, but Cut was tough—and big. He killed a lot of guys."

Stone changed the subject, not wanting to get into his past, his home. "I lied to you," he said with a smile, picking up the proffered glass of amber liquid that Rommel offered him. "I never saw that girl before in my life. I did it so I could get your attention. I've come here to work for you, Rommel,

join the Guardians. I'm smart, I'm tough, I got a thousand tricks up my sleeve. And I don't mind taking care of business when it comes time." He nodded and glanced at the body which lay like a fallen log near their feet.

"He killed Cut, man," one of the bikers croaked out, grinding his teeth together in fury. "What the hell you doing?" He started to rise from his seat, glaring at Stone as he reached into his jacket. But Rommel stood up in a flash, towering over the table with his awesome six-foot-eleven-inch 412-pound body as solid and seemingly unbreachable as a slab of steel. None of them dared challenge him.

"Cut was an asshole," Rommel roared. "I never liked that fucking guy. He smelled funny, he had at least three diseases that I know of, and worst of all, he's dead. Dead men can't fight or fuck." He laughed out a merry roar of black humor which the others couldn't help but join in. Stone grinned too and had the sudden mad vision, as he looked up at the immense physique, the scars and tattoos that covered Rommel's arms, that with his long beard and wide red face, he looked like nothing less than a barbarian St. Nicholas, a Santa Claus for the denizens of hell.

"I need some smart guys around here," the head biker said, sitting down again next to Stone. "You can't imagine how dumb some of these dudes are." He swung his head around at his men. "Can fight like motherfuckers but can only think like assholes. I got an empire to run here. The old days of just cruising around on our bikes and raping and having fun are over. It's more complicated now—we got to make our collections from all the stores, our drug sales on the street and to other cities. Then there's the books of the whorehouses. So many fucking numbers, figures to deal with."

He threw his hands over his face in mock horror. "You know how to add?"

"Add, subtract, multiply—I can do it all," Stone replied, finishing off the throat-burning drink.

"Then let's get the hell out of here. Got work to do!" Rommel slammed his hand down on the table so that those resting their elbows on it nearly flew off onto the floor. He put on his elephantine jacket and fitted the oak-sized arms covered with tattoos inside it. Thick steel chains hung down from each shoulder, and small skulls about the size of acorns and made of gold sat perched on each lapel, grinning out blinding smiles of wealth and dark power. He strode toward the front of the bar, Stone alongside him as the others threw their jackets and various weapons on and followed in a sulk behind.

"You know," said Rommel, towering over Stone as they headed out the door, "the only reason I let you live is because you remind me of myself years ago. I did the same thing you did. Exactly. Went up and killed the right hand to the main man. Now I'm the main man. You're smart. Don't get too smart 'cause I got my eye on you, got my eye on everybody. Believe me, I didn't get to be where I am by not knowing exactly what's going on. And if you and me had a go at it, I think you'd find the results a little different." He glanced down at Stone, letting him feel the full power of his eyes, his scarred face, his strength, his ability to crush every man he had ever faced.

"I was hoping for a long-term association," Stone said, his own face as unrevealing as the surface of cloudy ice. "Wouldn't have come all this way just to play games. I think

you'll see just how useful I can be—if you give me the chance."

"Sure, pal, I will give you the chance. Need some fresh blood in this fucking town. These guys talk about what drug they did this morning and which girls have syph and then pass out. Believe it or not, I'm something of an intellectual, a philosopher myself. Why, I've read books. In fact, I've developed my own particular brand of philosophy—Zen nihilistic hedonism—that I think combines the best of Nietzsche, Lao Tsu, and the Marquis de Sade. Helps me calm my nerves. And what's your philosophy of life, Stone?"

"I guess I'd have to call myself a student of death," Stone answered. "Studying all the myriad ways he manifests himself. For death teaches the living the lesson they'll never forget. And never remember either."

"Sounds heavy," Rommel said, looking sincerely at Stone. "Sounds real heavy. Me and you, man, we'll get a few ounces of methamfeddamine and talk this whole thing out—but later, after we have the Pleadings." He mounted his immense dinosaur of a bike—a 1500cc custom Harley which, with extra features—spikes pointing out from the sides of the wheels, swiveling machine gun on front and back, and armored side panels which rose up about two feet around the seat, forming a bulletproof barrier—must have weighed nearly a half ton. Only Rommel looked as if he could even move the thing. He pointed over to a red bike, low slung like a lizard and beat up to hell, that stood a few yards away.

"That was Cut's—it's yours now," Rommel shouted above the roar of the screaming, buffalo-sized machine atop which even the head biker looked small. "Everything that was Cut's is yours," he added cryptically and roared the engine of his

bike up so loud it sounded as if the thing were going to explode. Stone got his going, and then the rest of the Guardian top men ignited their engines into a deafening storm of noise that echoed up and down the main street. Suddenly Rommel pulled back on the throttle and tore out from the line into the center of Fairfax. He turned sharply, sliding his combat-booted foot along the concrete avenue and then, when the bike was pointing straight ahead, shot forward, somehow managing to execute a wheelie, pulling the back end of the half-ton bike a good three feet up into the air. Then he came down and shot along the main street, cracked here and there with tufts of grass growing through, hitting sixty within seconds. Stone followed suit, minus the acrobatics, and went after him as the rest of the bikers fell in one after the other, leaving little trails of smoke in the night air. They moved like a school of piranha, swimming a perfect straight line through the center of Denver as their eyes darted over the human fish that swam the nighttime streets, searching for any that might be worthy of their attention.

CHAPTER FIFTEEN

Rommel drove down Broadway, Denver's main thorough-fare, until he came to Colfax Avenue, where the band squealed around the corner at top speed. The state capitol, or what had once served as such—an exact miniature version of the nation's capitol, doric columns and all—stood straight ahead, its brilliant dome of hand-hammered gold leaf glistening from the cold rays of the moon. Motorcycles were parked or just thrown on their sides everywhere on the concrete walkways that surrounded the capitol. And from the flagpole that had once held the proud banners of the state of Colorado and the United States of America now swung only a body tied to the end of the hoist rope, badly decomposed, with but a few flakes of flesh left to be rotted away by bacteria and mold. The bones of its elbows and knees clicked sharply like bamboo wind chimes against the wooden pole as the stiff night

wind played its own grisly games with what remained of a man.

Rommel drove his bike right up the stairs of the building and onto the wide, curving terrace out front where he brought it finally to a putting stop. The guards, if they could be called that, were lying in a near drunken heap near the front door and looked up and tried to stand to attention as their leader rested his machine up on its kickstand and walked up the steps. He turned and smashed first one, then the other in the jaw with his inch-wide knuckles and yelled down at them as they lay in stupefied heaps, "If someone was attacking, assholes, we'd all be dead." Then he strode past them and inside the first-floor lobby of the immense building. Its once-shining marble walls and floors were marked with graffiti everywhere, obscene and mad.

Fuck till you die.

Razors are best.

Death is God.

I eat flesh.

Other such enobling sentiments had been scrawled in Magic Marker across not just the walls but the faces of the statues, the famous men and women of Colorado who had been preserved in bronze and steel a century before and now were subject to the indignities of having their sex organs drawn on their metallic bodies in reds and purples, huge and exaggerated, and things drawn into their mouths that in real life would assuredly not have been there.

Rommel stormed up the sweeping marble staircase to the second floor as Stone and the rest of the crew came tearing behind, trying to keep up with the man mountain. The immense oil paintings which had once graced the walls had long

since been ripped down. Inside the gold-gilded wooden frames had been hammered and glued pictures of Hitler, Mussolini, Charles Manson, and an occasional *Penthouse* or *Playboy* centerfold half faded but with breasts still pointing straight ahead with a hundred dirty handprints slapped down on top of them.

Rommel walked a few yards down the second-floor hallway and then through a pair of immense oak doors, where he made his way across a red carpet mottled with cigarette burns, straight for what Stone could only make out to be some sort of throne—a wide armchair covered in fake leopard skin with a drooping canopy of the same above it. The Guardian leader dropped down in it and smiled sweetly over at the leather-jacket-clad female with midnight-black hair trailing over her shoulders down to her waist who sat in a smaller but similar seat next to him and looked back with cold, angry eyes.

"Where the hell have you been? The court's been held up for an hour on account of you. There are people lined up around the block here to make their pleading."

"Bit of blood over at the bar," Rommel said, taking off his leather jacket, as the temperature was kept high in the gang headquarters. "Cut's dead, and we got a new member—Stone here." The woman looked over at Stone, who had stopped halfway down the rug and was staring around at the bizarre mixture of decorating styles —1980 Bureaucrat, Television Maharajah, and Biker Provincial—that the large mirrored room with chandeliers and hand-carved mahogany-paneled walls had been turned into.

"Where the hell did you come from?" the woman asked him with both scorn and attraction on her face. She was

beautiful. At least she looked as if she should be beautiful—with perfect ivory skin and high cheekbones, full, lush lips and a body beneath her skintight jeans and oversized gang jacket that a man might get lost in for years. But there was something hard about her. Something in the eyes that made him instantly wary. She looked as if she'd seen some terrible things—and wouldn't mind seeing them again.

"Just came," Stone answered, looking her squarely in the face, knowing she was giving him the once-over and not just with her eyes. "I heard that the Guardians always needed men who could kick ass, and that they had good dental benefits," Stone said with a smirk. "And that their women were the most beautiful. I want some action—something more interesting than taking off the stray car or two that passes for big time where I come from." Stone had learned weeks after entering puberty that every woman likes to be called beautiful, even if she could knock the teeth out of a man—as the one before him was obviously capable of doing. The rouge on her cheeks seemed to darken and her eyes swelled toward him.

"He's got a good rap," she said softly, looking over at Rommel and then back again to Stone.

"Stone, this here's Queenie. She's the Queen of the Slits—the girl branch of the Guardians. She's also my right hand—helps me run things. She's probably smarter than you or me put together—so watch out." Rommel took off his T-shirt, exposing a huge, muscular chest and arms the size of lampposts with tattoos of dragons and snakes covering everything above his waist. "And this here's Slash, Foot, Three Toes." The gang leader pointed around at his six top boys from the bar who had come in behind Stone and taken seats on the

floor around their leader. "No, Crash and Eddie." None of them looked up at Stone as the introductions were made except one—Eddie—and he looked as if he would have liked to slit Stone's throat on the spot.

"And Poet." a voice called out in a falsetto from behind Stone. He turned to see a legless, armless man with a body not larger than a watermelon riding in on some sort of electric wheelchair that he controlled by stabbing at the buttons on the side panel with the stumps of his arms. His face was contorted into a perpetual smile, as if the muscles had frozen in place, stretching it far out of shape. And yet smiling was the last thing one could imagine he wanted to be doing.

"And Poet." Rommel laughed as the wheel-bound deformity edged its way closer to the throne, hitting at the buttons on its wheelchair with arms only two inches long and streaked with throbbing red scar tissue. He brought the chair to an abrupt stop just feet from Stone.

"I am the asker of riddles," the deformity said. "The seeker of truths beyond truth."

"Why are you so ugly?" Stone asked, not cruelly but curious as to how the man had become so stricken.

"I'm ugly so you may feel beautiful, my whole friend," the limbless man said without a trace of anger. "I am but a mirror for those who see me so that they may feel joy that they are not me. As to how I became this way, I was stricken with cancer from the bombs—the radiation. Only my limbs were affected, and I was able to have them cut off before the cancer spread to the other parts of my body. I keep them still in bottles in my room, in formaldehyde. Perhaps you would like to see them sometime?"

"You should be touched," Rommel said, lighting up a

cigar-sized joint of Afghani gold. "Poet doesn't offer to show his appendages to everyone." Two of the Guardians standing as close as they could came to attention on each side of the wide doorway, suddenly squeezed motorcycle horns they were holding in their hands and yelled out simultaneously, "The Court of His Honor, General Rommel, is now in session."

Stone sat down on the far side of Queenie in another of the spring-popping armchairs that the bikers seemed to love as she gave him a quick look of lust and murder, both sentiments twinkling from her beautiful green eyes.

"Yes, yes, bring them on," Rommel said, sucking hard on the smoke and leaning back in his chair so that an immense fart exploded out through the chamber. The guards led a man in, his hands tied together. He was asthmatic, gasping so hard that it looked as if he might spill his beans at any moment.

"Charge," one of the guards read, looking down at a piece of dirty paper. "Stealing receipts from official Guardian drug runs. He's just a messenger boy, but his hands got greedy. Was taking a nickel out of every dollar."

"What do you have to say for yourself, asshole?" Rommel grunted, blowing smoke in the man's face.

"I—I—I—" the low-level hustler stuttered, unable to speak. He knew the kind of punishments they were capable of.

"What do you think, beautiful one?" the biker asked, leaning toward Queenie.

"Kill him," she said, bored. "It's hardly an interesting case or one worthy of time." The limbless one slammed his stumps against the buttons of his chair, swiveling around toward Rommel.

"What is the sound of no hands clapping?" Poet asked rhetorically through his contorted grin. He waited only a

said. "Not too many folks wants to die. Do you have any womenfolk?" the head biker asked the accused.

"Yeah, got me a sister," he answered nervously, his eyes unable to meet the full gaze of the four-hundred-pound tattooed judge who sat half naked, staring down at him. "She's sick. She lives up in the hills and—"

"Dwarf, what do you think?" Rommel asked, turning to the pasty, oval-shaped thing in the steel wheelchair.

"A tooth for a tooth, an orifice for an orifice, Your Honor," Poet whispered, leaning over in his chair, which he had pulled up right alongside Rommel's so that his thin lips almost touched the bearded face.

"Yes, I see your point. All right, I'm ready to pass sentence," the big biker said, taking another slug of the double-distilled gin, his favorite drink. "Have this crying slug on the floor here fuck the accused's sister—and then kill her. That's fair, isn't it?" he beamed, looking around at his top aides.

"More than fair," the seated Guardians replied in bored tones.

"Take him off then," Rommel said, waving his hand.

"Cut off his cock," Queenie added in a stiletto of a whisper.

"Yes—" The biker hesitated for a second as they dragged the suddenly screaming piece of filth away. "And cut his cock off too—but let him keep it as a souvenir."

"Excellent, excellent." Poet laughed through gritted teeth as he tried futilely to slap his stumps together in applause.

"Yes, we are doing rather well tonight, aren't we?" Rommel said, smiling. He looked around benignly at his drunken top men and then at Stone, feeling most proud of the way he meted out justice.

"Charge," the door guard screamed at the top of his lungs.

"Stolen cow." He walked in two men and on the end of a rope a large milking cow which ambled dumbly along, glancing around the floor as if there might be grass to eat.

"This bastard stole my cow. My only cow," one of the men said, a timid, curly-haired fellow who looked as if he had once been a schoolteacher or social worker now reduced to much harder times.

"My cow," the other one said, jumping in front of the first. "It was my fucking cow. Had her since she was size of a pig."

"Either of you got proof?" Rommel asked. "Papers? Documents?"

"No," they both answered simultaneously, looking fearfully down at their own feet, unable to meet the faces of the bikers who stared at them as if they were bugs.

"Cut off its cock," Queenie said with bored exasperation without looking up from doing her nails. "Cut off their cocks, cut off all men's cocks."

"You see that, Stone?" Rommel said with a deep belly laugh. "You've got to be careful with her. She's so tough she don't want no man fucking her—but she needs it 'cause she's a woman. So whoever she screws, she has to cut off their cock and then kill him. That's why you won't see none of my boys messing with her. Me neither. If she starts looking at you, you might as well get yourself measured for a pine box." Queenie smiled ever so sweetly at Stone, and he knew he was in trouble.

"Well, you'll be happy to know," Rommel said, rising from his seat with a broad smile as he addressed the two men, "that we've had this kind of complaint before—and we've worked out a perfect solution." He turned to one of

the door guards. "Get me the saw, the big one—the new one," the biker commanded. Within a minute the Guardian returned with a heavy-duty gasoline-powered chain saw with a three-foot blade.

"Bring the cow over here," Rommel ordered the guards, who dragged the big white-and-black-spotted creature to the center of the chamber. They held it—one by the ears, the other by the tail, pulling as hard as they could in opposite directions. Rommel started up the wood-cutting device and lowered it toward the suddenly terrified animal, which didn't like the screaming sound at all. It let out a wild moo, and then as the blade bit into its back the sound changed into the most unearthly bellow Stone had ever heard—an animal sound but filled with an almost conscious pain, as if the animal understood what a terrible thing was happening to it.

The saw slid right down through the cow's thick hide, then through the spine, the ribs, and on through the stomach. It took only seconds and then the animal, cut cleanly in two, a final moo still gurgling through its lips, fell to the floor in two bloody piles, its inner organs squirming out in all directions, propelled by the blood that squirted from the severed arterial connections.

"Excellent cut," Poet laughed, squirming around in his chair.

Rommel stepped back and surveyed his handiwork. "There—you may each take your cow." The two men, too frightened to protest, began dragging the huge, dripping mounds of cow by the legs and pulling for all they were worth. They left a red trail out the door and down the Persian-carpeted stairs.

CHAPTER
SIXTEEN

The Pleadings, as they were called, where those unfortunate enough to stand accused pleaded their cases and their lives before the Court of the Guardians of Hell, went on for nearly two hours, with Rommel carrying out justice according to his own twisted laws of logic. At last he clapped his hands together and said, "The court is closed for the night. Clear the building." The guards slammed shut the big oak doors to the room and took the remainder of those who had been waiting back to their jail cells and hovels. The next and perhaps final chapter in the story of their lives would be written another day.

"Bring drugs, girls, food," Rommel bellowed out at the top of his lungs. "I'm tired. I've worked too hard today. I must have pleasure or I'll die." The faces of his biker crew came to life from out of a dulled lethargy as slaves appeared out of nowhere, carrying trays of pills and marijauna, which

they passed around to the Guardians. The limbless dwarf yelled at the slaves to put a red and blue pill in his mouth, shaking his stumps furiously until one came over and slid the pill between the forever-frozen smile on the tight little face.

"Girls, girls, come here, you hot little bitches," Rommel snorted happily as a dozen or so of them came running out, stark naked, and jumped into the laps and arms of the bikers, who grabbed them without a lot of what in prewar days had been called foreplay and began doing their thing with them. There was even a girl for Poet—an amputee, but of normal height. Both of her arms were gone, but her legs worked fine. She leaned against the edge of the chair, pushing her chest against the egg-shaped creature and began kissing the top of his nearly bald head. The slug of a man struggled violently, trying to work his way out of his pants so she could get to the twisted organ that lay within.

Another girl, very young and once lovely, although now bruised around the face, her eyes blackened, lay her head on Stone's lap. He put his arms around her firm young body, but he kept an eye on the goings-on around the room. He saw Queenie staring back at him with a look that only a spider could have for a fly, her eyes big and wet, her breasts rising, pushing out hard against her T-shirt, as if reaching for him. But he'd be the dumbest man alive to make it with her—he would be signing his own death sentence.

"Hey, guess what time it is," Rommel said with slurred speech from the effect of the pills and gin he kept slugging down as he took his mouth off the chest of one of the teenage girls who sat naked on his right leg. "It's initiation time, man. Bring out the special tray," the biker yelled to a servant standing behind his polyester-leopard-skin throne. Within sixty

seconds a servant wearing a white chef's uniform walked over to Stone carrying a tray in his hand. He leaned over and lifted the stainless-steel lid and Stone looked inside. A heart, steaming and dripping with bloody juices, sat in the middle.

"What the hell is that?" Stone asked nervously.

"That's stage two of your initiation into the Guardians." Rommel laughed. "It's Cut's heart, Stone. Remember, I said everything of his belonged to you now. Well, that's part of him. Stage one—to become one of us is to kill a man. You already done that. Stage two—eat his heart. If you can't take the heat, get up and leave now," Rommel said, his face growing cold, devoid of laughter. "I'll let you live. Every man has to do it. To be a Guardian you can't be like other men."

Stone kept a grip on himself as his mind went wild as a short-circuiting computer. He remembered his father telling him stories of having eaten beetles, worms, dead animals found on trails in the years he fought in Asia. Even VC flesh once when he had been lying with a broken leg at the bottom of a ravine, unable to move for nearly a week and only the man he had killed next to him for food. "A man's got to do anything to survive, Martin. If he's got a mission—that's what matters. What he does to carry it out is unimportant." Well, Stone had a mission—to save April. And the only way he was going to have the slightest chance of finding her would be through the Guardians. They controlled all the whore-houses. He reached for the tray and then for the fork which the servant handed him. At least it was high protein—Dad would be proud.

When he saw that the meal had been completed, Rommel dragged himself from his fondling of the two teens and walked

over to Stone, slapping him hard on the back. "There you go. Not so bad, right? How'd the bastard taste? Better than he smelled in life, I'll wager, or you wouldn't still be standing." Stone had no reply.

"Now's the next part," the gang leader said, pulling out his long hunting knife and holding it toward Stone, who flinched, suddenly thinking he had walked into a trap and they were just going to kill him. But Rommel placed the blade at the top of Stone's arm and dug it in about a half inch, pulling the knife hard all the way down to his wrist. The arm poured out a stream of blood, and Stone felt a rush of dizziness for a second as he saw his body fluids rushing from him. Rommel rolled up his own sleeve and placed the tip of the blade against his flesh. Stone could see that he had been cut numerous times before, as long welts ran up and down his arm like red canals. He dug the knife in and pulled it evenly all the way down without grimacing in the slightest.

Rommel grabbed Stone's arm and slammed it against his so the blood of the two mingled together. Then, with his eyes tightly closed as if in a trance, he began chanting, "Your blood with my blood. Now we are the same blood. The dark blood. The blood without mercy. We are Guardians of Hell. We guard hell, Stone. Guard the gates of hell so that they do not close. And in return we take what we want. You can have all that you want, Stone. But know that now you are of our blood. You must protect our blood. And you must die if you betray our blood. Say it. Say, I am a Guardian of Hell."

"I am a Guardian of Hell," Stone said, not without fear, but his fear was of the words, not the pain, for somewhere inside him the thought that he was blaspheming against God with that oath filled him with more reluctance than anything

he had had to do in the last few days. But he knew inside himself that it wasn't real. Knew that he was a pretender in this land of those who loved pain and death. He had to know that, had to always remember that no matter what happened. For he knew that even the strongest men had crumbled under the twin seductions of great power mixed with absolute immorality, enabling them to do anything and to carry the blackest deeds to infinite perfection.

"Welcome to the darkness," Rommel said, stepping back and pouring gin on his and Stone's arms. The liquor stung like pure fire, and Stone knew that it was a good antiseptic and let the pain take his mind from the words of the chant which had left his spine trembling with a fear deeper than the mind can go.

"And, well, that's just about it," Rommel said, taking three great gulps of the clear alcohol.

"Just about? What the hell else could there be?" Stone asked.

"Shots, Stone. We each get one good shot. You know— just to welcome you to our happy organization. It's really just an expression of our affection. Come on, you assholes," Rommel yelled over to his men, who were already deeply entwined with their girls as they rolled drunkenly around the floor. He walked over to them and pulled them bodily from their drugged-out bags of flesh. "Fuck later—got to welcome a new member," Rommel commanded them, dragging them half naked across the floor.

"You first," he said, pointing to one of them whose name Stone had already forgotten but whose face he would never forget as it drew close, hard and mean, with a look of sheer murder. The biker drew back his fist as Stone suddenly re-

alized this meant each man could hit him anywhere. He braced himself, fighting the urge to block each shot, and waited. The blow caught him just the side of the neck as the short but bull-shouldered biker went slightly off target. Stone spun with the blow and felt an almost numbing pain run along his shoulder like a snake and then back up again. Stone faced forward again, and another coffeepot-sized fist drew back and came like a meteor right for his nose. This one caught him square in the middle of the face and knocked him straight back, sending electric flashes through his skull, as if a whole row of floodlights were being turned rapidly on and off inside his brain.

He somehow made himself walk forward a few steps to where the next Guardian was waiting in line. He was doing this for April. He had to remember that. It was all for her. She was the only one who was left and— He was slammed backward, this time by a shot that caught him right under the chin and lifted him inches in the air before sending him to the ground. He felt himself blacking out and then coming to again as the picture tube of his brain blinked like mad.

After that he didn't really remember much of what happened. He was down. Then he was getting up. Then there was a fist, then another. And it felt as if his face was gone. Then he remembered Queenie. Her foot heading for his groin. And then he remembered nothing.

CHAPTER
SEVENTEEN

When he awoke, his jaw felt as if it might be broken. But he was glad to be alive. He was never sure with these people whether they were for real or just playing with him. Somehow he knew he didn't have a lot of time. He had to find April—fast. He opened his eyes to let in the sunlight from the wide-arching windows along one side of the chamber and rose to his elbows from his position on the carpeted floor where he had been lying since he fell from the final blow. The place was a wreck—tables overturned, broken bottles and glasses, a few patches of dried blood. They'd really had some fun after knocking Stone out cold.

"They're all sleeping now—in the bedrooms," a voice spoke out from the shadows a few feet away. Then the wheel-chair edged forward into a shaft of sunlight and the pale face of the limbless Poet appeared, smiling its hideous, eternal grin. "They'll sleep until midafternoon and then rise," the

oval of flesh said in that unearthly, high-pitched voice that sounded more like the nonhuman cackle that a ventriloquist might project into a dummy than the voice of a man. "It's always like that. The Guardians live by night and sleep in the day—like vampires, werewolves, and other assorted beings."

"Well, I see you're up bright and early," Stone groaned as he rose to his trembling legs, and had to lean against a table for a second to support himself as everything grew foggy and dense. They had beaten the shit out of him, the bastards, and this was the second time. But it would all be repaid— with interest.

"I never sleep," Poet said. "Occasionally, I drift off into a half sleep, a twilight where my thoughts mesh with the thoughts of the world around me. But these are more night-mares than dreams. That is all I am capable of—nightmares. Thus I avoid being in the state that produces them. I'm sure were you in my shoes you would find that you have not feet to put in them."

"Sorry I asked." Stone grimaced, as he didn't feel like getting even more depressed this morning than he already was.

"I would have hit you last night," Poet went on, "along with the rest. But as you can see"—he spun both stumps around and then thrust them forward in mock punches—"it's hard for me to actually reach anything." There was something about the half-man that sickened Martin, made it hard for him to even look at it or be near it, as if he might somehow catch whatever had made it evolve into its present form. He started for the door.

"Oh, by the way—that jacket there on the floor—it's

yours," Poet said. "You're official now. A Guardian. You'll find it will give you much power—and also make you the target of certain jealous elements."

"I'm already the target of just about every living thing I pass," Stone answered, slipping into the raw-smelling leather jacket with the huge skull-on-H-bomb freshly painted on the back.

"Tell me, Martin Stone," Poet went on, steering his wheelchair around in a jerking circle toward Stone. "Why. are you really here? What are you searching for?"

"How—how do you know my first name?" Stone asked, spinning around.

"I know all that passes through Denver. This is my world—the perversions, the murders, the double crosses. Nothing escapes my attention. For example, you are not what you seem, though just what game you are playing is not totally clear to me yet. But give it time. By tonight or tomorrow I guarantee I will have you pegged and squirming like a butterfly under a pin, and then I shall use my knowledge to blackmail you as I have blackmailed all the others. Why do you think they even keep me around? I have too much on every one of them for them to dare let anything happen to me. Soon you will be in my grip as well—though I haven't yet decided the price."

"Something to look forward to," Stone grumbled as he strode angrily out the door. The stump thing was lucky he didn't knock its fucking head off and add one more jagged ending to a body that hardly needed any additions. He headed downstairs, almost passing out on the wide marble steps as he felt suddenly light-headed and off balance. He'd have to

go slowly for a while—give all the loose bolts a chance to fall back into place.

He headed outside where the piercing sunshine and crisp, throat-burning air immediately woke him up and shot some energy through his system. He walked for a few minutes to get things moving inside again and then stopped in a run-down diner for coffee and pie. The city seemed to still have business—groceries, liquor stores, even a movie theater or two. But all of them were dirty, dark little places whose customers walked in and out of their doors with their heads bent over and their eyes darting from side to side as if expecting something to attack them at any moment. It was a dreary, gray world, nothing like the city he had known before the war.

Stone walked up and down half the streets of Denver that day, stopping in every strip joint, every whorehouse he passed, trying to track down April. He kept asking for the youngest, blondest hookers they had, and though several looked like his sister, none of them was. It made him feel sicker and sicker to see what they had done to so many innocent girls. Girls sixteen, twelve, all the way down to seven or eight. The city had apparently become one of the main bordellos of the West—all run by the Guardians and their female enforcement squads, the Slits. Denver was now the city where anything went. Where anything could be bought, fucked, or killed for a price. The town for those so jaded that only the mixture of blood and screams could bring on climax. And the faces of the girls Stone looked at throughout the afternoon showed that use—their faces smashed and smashed again, their young, firm bodies torn and covered with welts and scars from previous customers. Stone could see that one's

career in the business was short-lived. And then what—killed, sold, ground up into food for one of their restaurants? He could believe anything now about any of them. A worse lot of human beings had never walked the face of the earth.

In the twentieth or twenty-fifth—he had long since lost count—decrepit little "love motel" that Stone entered, he at last got a lead from an old fat woman at the front desk, who was talkative and ready to blab about anything.

"Well, if she was really young and pretty, she wouldn't be in any of these places nohow, anyway," the buxom, heavily rouged and lipsticked hooker said with a constant, automatic come-hither smile planted on her face from years of trying to talk men into buying her body. "They probably would have taken her to the Western Tower—save her for the games."

"The what?" Stone asked.

"You're a Guardian and you don't know what—"

"I'm new here," Stone growled. "Don't get me mad." He'd have to play it the way a real biker would—mean and nasty all the way. He pulled his blade out and looked at her. "Tell me—explain it to me. Don't leave out anything."

"Sure, sure, Mr. Guardian," the woman croaked, putting her hands up in front of her. "Sorry, didn't mean to—"

"Talk, talk, idiot," he yelled, waving the knife at her.

"They take all the virgins—and near virgins—especially the ones who aren't too marked up, and put 'em in this tower—actually this half-fallen office building in the middle of town. Then when the games are over tomorrow night—"

"Games? What games?" He flickered the blade again.

"The—the games that you and all your Guardian brothers play each year to see who's the best—the Toughest Mother-

fucker in the West competition. Fighting, shooting—got everything, from what I've heard. Of course I've never been to them."

"And these start tomorrow?" Stone asked.

"Sure do," the hooker said. "Why, boys been pulling up from over the nearby states for days now. That's why the streets are so full of bikes. They'll be looking for action tonight and tomorrow night—town will be boiling over."

"Thanks," Stone said abruptly, heading out the door and straight toward the Western Tower. But it was clear the moment he reached the cylindrical building that it wasn't going to be that easy. Machine-gun emplacements surrounded the building, manned by nearly two dozen men, and these looked a lot more alert than the ones who had guarded the gang's headquarters in the state capitol building. Stone walked slowly up to the cigar-shaped structure which had only twenty of its original thirty-eight stories remaining—the rest apparently having been blown off in some sort of fire and explosion that the building had suffered years before, as the top few levels were still charred and blackened.

"Don't come no closer, brother," a voice yelled out from behind one of the sandbags. "Every guy who's come into town comes riding by here to see what we got. Well, you can't see. You want to get a peek or a sniff, you just going to have to win one of the games. We got orders to shoot, so fuck off. Don't want to kill one of my own today."

Stone sauntered off and made a slow circumference of the building from across the street. The machine-gun crews noticed him, but as long as he stayed out of range they seemed

to not get too riled up. They had the place completely sealed off. It would be virtually impossible to smash his way in. Well, that made it simple. He'd just have to win one of the games, so he could get the prize of his own sister.

CHAPTER
EIGHTEEN

Stone made his way back to the gang headquarters in the state capitol to find Rommel conducting his court between snorts of ether that one of his boys had dug up from somewhere. He'd listen to a case, take a deep sniff of the powerful liquid gas, and go into a swoon from which he would scream out the sentence in a state of drugged-out ecstasy. The bikers greeted Stone with the closest thing they'd given him to smiles since he'd been there. Rommel, No, Eddie, the dwarf, and especially Queenie actually seemed glad to see him. Having gone through the initiation and now being a Guardian apparently put him on a different footing. He was a member of the club now, the most exclusive—and deadly—club in America.

Stone watched the absurd legal proceedings for about an hour and then, before the nightly orgies began, slipped away to a back room in the immense building. He needed rest,

time to heal. Tomorrow would be the most important day of his life—and April's too. By tomorrow night she would be free, and they could leave this hellhole. But before he left, Stone would implement some of what he had spent years learning. The student of death was about to become the teacher.

He woke early, the sun just peering in through the small window of his third-floor room. No one had found him, and he hadn't even heard the screams from the nightly festivities at the front end of the mansion, so at last he'd had a good night's sleep. The rest made his body feel greatly healed as well, his jaw not even swollen anymore. He dressed and then took out his firepower, the .44 and the Uzi autopistol, and stripped both of them down to their metal underwear, cleaning every crevice, every lever and release. Then he snapped them together again, reloaded them, and eased them back into their holsters. He checked the mini-.38 secreted in his boot and a few other little tricks he had hidden here and there. Then he put on the jacket, looking in the wall mirror at the garish painting on the back.

"Always wanted a varsity jacket." He smiled at his reflection, noticing for the first time that he had aged. Just in the weeks he had been out of the shelter he had changed. He had seemed not to age inside the bunker for those five years, as if his body were in a state of suspended animation, waiting for something real to bring it to life again. But now there were lines around his eyes, his mouth. His face seemed more pulled in, tougher looking, and his dusky blonde hair was darker. How could it not be? A person was what he saw around him, nothing more, nothing less. And he was walking through a world that had nothing but rot and dissolution permeating every cell of it.

Stone found Cut's beat-up bike outside and headed out to the domed stadium at the edge of town where the Guardian Olympics were being held. The competition he had decided to compete in—Handgun Target and Speed Shooting—wasn't scheduled to begin until two, but he wanted to see what the competition was like. The place was filled to the brim with bikers by the time he arrived, motorcycles parked everywhere around the outskirts of the six-acre site that had once been a sports training complex for the Denver Broncos football team, complete with mini domed stadium in the middle. Stone walked into the structure, which was much in need of repair—large portions of the fiberglass overhead had fallen out, and immense cracks covered what was left.

It was clear that no maintenance work was being done on any of the buildings or machinery in Denver. Was it that way everywhere around the country? Stone wondered. Everything just slowly falling apart, nothing new being built, and no one even remembering how to repair whatever the hell was left? The whole country would just sort of slither its way back down into darkness. Not with a bang—in fact, no one would even notice. But each year there would be less materials, fewer machines that functioned, fewer books, fewer ideas. And then one day there would be none. And the savages who were left would stare at one another and pick up a rusted rifle and use it as a club and the whole damned thing would start all over again.

I'm always so optimistic, Stone thought with a grim smile as he headed down the walkway and joined the crowds of bikers who were streaming into the partially collapsed building. Everywhere bikers were competing in contests of brute strength, brute force, brute madness. Stone stopped and

watched as two men faced off and came at each other from a distance of about ten feet. They lowered their heads as they accelerated and slammed their skulls into one another like mountain goats in mating season. Men lay all around the ground, their faces and scalps drenched in red. No one tended to them. Casualties in these games fended for themselves.

He walked on to the next crowd and squeezed in. A weight-lifting competition was being held, with bikers stripped to the waist, flexing their muscles and screaming out at the tops of their lungs as they mentally prepared themselves for their immense loads. One man suddenly stepped forward, ready to try. He reached down and gripped tremendous hands around the middle of a ten-foot-long piece of plumbing pipe, at each end of which hung four automobile tires, for a total of eight. They had already worked their way up through two, four, and six tires, and only five men were left. Each of them was huge—three of them even larger than Rommel, with biceps that measured in feet, not inches, broad chests wider than the motorcycles they drove, and a rainbow of tattoos of dragons, women, and symbols of fascism covering their bodies in a net of sweating color.

The man set under the great weight, which Stone estimated to be at least seven hundred pounds, and pushed up with all his might. Every vein straining at maximum elevation, the man huffed and puffed, looking as if the outer flesh of his body could not contain the explosive pressures within. But somehow the biker got the thing over his head, held it there three seconds, and then let it fall forward with a great slam into the dirt. He threw his hands into the air and let out a roar of victory.

Next Stone watched the knife-fighting contests. Men slashed

and stabbed at one another in all kinds of styles. Killing blows weren't allowed, but everything else was. And the contestants were covered with long cuts, streaks of bright red crisscrossing every part of their bodies, marks that they wore proudly— badges of psychotic courage. Stone was glad he had chosen a different competition. This looked as if it could rapidly use up all a person's available blood supply.

In the center of the stadium—what had been the football field—some sort of motorcycle competition was being held. Stone made his way over, drawn by the roar of dozens of engines revving up, and watched as the two teams faced off about thirty feet apart in the center of the field. Its ancient football yardage lines were still dimly visible in the brown grass beneath them. A referee fired a Thompson submachine gun into the air, and the game was on. Stone strained forward as another ref threw something from a bag into the space between the two teams and then jumped backward out of the way. The teams—one with red flags, the other with black tied to their handlebars—shot forward at full speed in pursuit of the rolling ball. Bikes crashed headlong into one another, Guardians flew off every which way. The first rider to reach the ball swatted at it with what Stone could make out to be a tennis racket, giving the object a good whack so that it flew down the field.

Both teams pursued, bikes coming in from every direction, rackets swinging wildly at everything that came near them. But the man with the ball was good—and fast—as he steered his bike downfield toward where Stone was standing, slamming the racket every ten feet or so to keep the thing rolling. The biker approached the goal line, where another biker waited, his black motorcycle guarding the net behind him. The of-

fensive man pulled his arm all the way back and swung down and the ball rocketed into the air and toward the end zone. Stone watched with a sudden sickening feeling as he saw that the game ball, which was flying past him just yards away, had eyes and a mouth and a hole that had once been a nose. The bastards were playing with a human head.

The goalie, a man so gargantuan that even his 1400cc custom cruiser sank beneath his five hundred pounds of sumo-wrestler physique, reached under his jacket and fired up at the descending object. The head flew into a spray of finely ground bone fragments which settled down to the moist earth and sank invisibly into the ground below. The referee pulled out another head from his apparently inexhaustible supply, threw it between the two teams, and they went at it again, screaming and cursing as they tried to swat the hard object to victory.

Stone was grateful when he heard the scratchy, static-filled announcement come over the single functioning speaker of the PA system that the pistol challenge was about to begin at the north end of the stadium. He pulled back through the crowd as the headhunters went at it, much to the delight of the whistling and clapping fans of the subtle sport.

Stone walked up to the firing range and looked at the human targets which had been set up at various distances— blue-faced corpses nailed by their wrists and ankles to four-by-eight-foot sheets of raw plywood at which Guardians were already firing their weapons. Bullets of every caliber tore into swollen and dead flesh as if flies were taking bites out of it. Pieces of skull slowly were eaten away; arms riddled at the shoulder fell off onto the ground. But the bikers just kept firing and reloading. Stone wasn't quite sure how the judges—

three older bikers, their beards a little gray around the edges—
were keeping score, but they kept looking up and then scrib-
bling away in pads of paper.

At last it was Stone and two other bikers' turn to fire.
Fresh bodies were placed up in the plywood frame as the last
batch had turned to mush under the five-minute barrage of
the shooters and dribbled down the front of the bullet-riddled
wood like red varnish. But Stone wouldn't need five minutes
to take care of his cadaver—not even five shots.

He stood with his Ruger Redhawk .44 mag held out nearly
straight in front of him with his right hand while the left hand
braced around the wrist, his elbow resting tight against his
chest. It was his father's style—out of fashion now, but it
was what he had learned and it would have to do. The two
other Guardians looked over curiously at Stone's thirteen-
and-a-half-inch blunderbuss, with its gleaming chromed frame.
The thing looked more like it should be mounted in an artillery
unit than used in a pistol competition. One biker held a six-
gun, Texas style—.38 Colt Special, pearl handles and all—
and the other a Charter Arms Explorer firing .22 long, with
its distinctive tubular twelve-inch barrel. Stone was ready to
go against anything with his Hawk. He knew what it could
do.

"You understand the rules," one of the judges yelled out.
"Whoever has destroyed most of the body within one minute—paying close attention to vital areas—will win the most
points. Ready, set, *go*."

The Guardians to the left of Stone opened up, pulling their
fingers again and again on the triggers as big gouges appeared
in the fresh corpses. Stone took his time, sighted down the
Red Dot Aimset until the tiny circle was resting right between

the target's hard black eyes. He squeezed the trigger gently and the big pistol bucked back in his hand like a thing alive. The 240-grain slug left the smoking muzzle at 1,350 feet per second and tore into the center of the head, blasting it into smoke and gristle. And when the smoke cleared, there was nothing there but a limp body with no top. As if not wanting to keep the miserable remnant of a man in a state of semi-dissection, Stone sighted and fired three times quickly, moving a foot down the body each time. The three magnum slugs ripped into the body within tenths of a second of one another. The top one blasted the chest apart, sending the rib cage flying off in two directions. The middle shot tore into the stomach, spinning it around it like a propeller sending everything within it into an instantaneous eruption of red stew. The final shot hit the pelvis, disintegrating the bone into shards.

There was silence for a moment as even the other two shooters stopped to see what had happened. There was nothing left on Stone's board except stains and the two legs, which seemed to shiver and almost dance inside their blood-coated overalls. Then they tumbled free of the wall, falling down in separate directions as if off to take a constitutional.

The judges had no choice but to give Stone the award. No other man had caused so much damage with so few shots. An hour later he was standing in the center of the stadium along with the ten other winners. The crowd of scar-faced, drunken bikers cheered the men to the skies. These were their heroes—the masters of bringing blood into the world.

CHAPTER NINETEEN

So far, so good, Stone thought as he quickly headed out from the stadium. He would get to the Western Tower before the others and collect his prize. Maybe this whole damned thing was going to be easier than he thought. But the moment a man thinks that things are going well, reality will inevitably lend a fist to smash him in the face and say different.

Stone had just reached his motorcycle when figures jumped suddenly from several doorways. Before he could even pull a weapon, a piano wire was thrown around his throat, pulling him straight backward at the same instant another strand of the cutting wire slipped around his ankles, pulling him off his feet. He tried to fight back, but there was no time as he began falling unconscious from the garrote. Just before he slipped under, he thought he saw Queenie's face looking down at him with a lewd expression.

When he awoke, he was lying on a bed, his arms and legs

tied with the same piano wire to a steel frame beneath the mattress. His neck hurt as if he had just been guillotined, and he could feel a ring of dried blood around where the wire had sunk in a good quarter inch—but at least he still had something up there. A little harder and he would have been the game ball in their next round of motorcycle polo. He raised his head, grimacing slightly as a stab of pain raced through the wound around his throat. He was in a room that was totally empty but for the bed he lay in—and the ten women who stood around the foot of the bed, staring down at him silently and intently.

He must have made a strange face as he jerked back startled when he saw them, for the women burst into raucous laughter, screwing their faces up as they mocked his expression.

"Don't be afraid, brother Stone," Queenie said, her hands on her hips. "Most men would pay a ransom to be trapped alone with ten beautiful women with only one thing on their minds." She walked around the bed, dressed in a skintight leather outfit with portions cut out around her breasts, buttocks, and pubic area so that all her charms were freely displayed. "Come now, don't you find me the least attractive?"

"Attractive, yes," Stone said, looking up at her as his eyes fanned the room, searching desperately for some way out. "Like a flame is to a moth. Only problem is, I'll be dead as soon as I touch you."

"Not as soon as. You'll get to enjoy your arousal. Isn't that another of man's most fervent wishes, to die in the midst of orgasm? That is what I offer you. Only, I will bring you to the very peak of sensation and then spice it with the edge of my blade." She took a long, scalpellike knife from a

scabbard at her side and slid it along his sweat shirt, cutting just deeply enough to slice the thick material in two for a length of several inches. "See, it is so sharp. I love sharp things. I love the way they cut flesh. It's so easy to cut flesh, Stone. Do you know that? How you just put the point in and it seems to sink in all by itself, as if it wanted to go in. Do you know what I mean?" She looked at him fervently, her cheeks growing flushed from obvious sexual excitement.

"Oh, yes, I never feel happier than when cutting things with a nice sharp blade," Stone said, looking up at her. He tried to get a glimpse of the others too. There were nine more of them—all dressed in the same black leather jackets and pants that the men wore, only skintight and with rhinestones along the sleeves and seams. And on the backs of their jackets the words THE SLITS were written in blood-red in jagged letters. They looked tough enough to take out most men, with brawny shoulders and faces that had been pushed in a few times too many. And every one of them was staring at his muscular young body with undisguised lust.

"What is the sound of a penis rising?" a voice asked from out of the shadows at the back of the room. Stone turned his head, knowing before he saw the hideous oval shape that it was Poet. The stumped dwarf, poking at the buttons on his electric wheelchair, moved forward until he was at the foot of the bed. The eternal smile on the thing's face seemed more twisted than ever, as if the dwarf's teeth would surely have to pop out like so many marbles onto the floor. "Its owner's screams when it is severed from his body," Poet said, answering his own Zen koan of violence.

"So you're here too!" Stone muttered with a smirk. "I

should have known the biggest freak in town wouldn't miss the freak show."

"I'm invited to all the best parties," the dwarf answered, rolling around the bed as if looking for a good vantage point from which to view the sexual carnage about to unfold. "Why, I dare say, my presence is de rigeuer at any function, be it sex or murder, or the event just couldn't be called a success."

Queenie walked over until she was standing by the head of the bed. She leaned down and tenderly kissed his lips and whispered, "You and I will make such sweet music together, Stone. I'll kiss you as you die. I'll taste your soul as it flees, drink your final breath of life into my mouth. The taste of a lover at the instant of death is an intoxicating drug. Once sampled—an addiction." She lifted her lips away from his ear and stood up, and at the same instant Stone felt a burning sensation sear across his chest. He looked down. She had cut him, just lightly—a lover's caress before the main course.

She seemed to fall into a trance, spouting her poetry of homicidal romanticism as she walked around the room. Stone knew he'd better make whatever moves he had left before she cut off something he needed. She reached the far wall as she walked in a wide, dramatic circle and went into a nearly incomprehensible soliloquy about the need for life to be affirmed through death and the merging of pain and pleasure.

Although tied tightly, Stone had about a foot of slack on the wire. Moving slowly, he slid his right arm down while he pulled his right leg up. If he could just reach it—just a few seconds. He had just gotten his hand down to the heel of the boot and found the tiny lever that released it when a voice called out from across the room. "He's got something." They rushed toward him en masse.

"Christ," Stone groaned at the very second he pushed the lever. A small push-dagger knife fell into the palm of his hand. The three-inch double-sided blade sat in the center of a small bone handle, giving him a strong grip. With just the strength of his wrist, as he had barely any leverage, he whipped the blade down on the wire around his right leg. It sliced through just as the first of the Slits reached the foot of the bed. Stone ripped the blade the other way, releasing the left foot, and then kicked out with his boot as a hand came down to grab him. The boot connected with an elbow, cracking it, and the grabbing arm flew backward. With hands coming in from every side, he swung the blade up in a wide circle and whacked it into both wires that bound his wrists. They parted with satisfying snaps, and he was free.

Stone jumped down onto the floor, waving the blade in front of him, trying to force back the closing circle of women. "Come on now, I don't want to have to hurt any of you." They drew close but stopped just short of the flashing blade. They had no reason to get cut.

"You're not going anywhere," Queenie said, jumping in his way, hefting her scalpel. Her eyes were wild, like those of a hungry cat, a creature that hadn't eaten for days.

"Out of the way, sugar," Stone said. "I've got to meet someone very special to me."

"You still don't understand, do you, you pitiful fool?" the statuesque woman asked contemptuously. "You die in here." She lunged toward him with the scalpel, slicing at his face. Stone blocked the arm with a strike from his forearm, pushing her whole body to the side. He stepped in and sank the blade of the push dagger up under her rib cage, straight into the heart. He pulled the hand back again and stepped away.

Queenie looked surprised, then angry. Then her whole face seemed to soften as she slid to the ground and realized she was going to die. Stone swore her lips formed the word "thanks," and then she was gone, the pierced heart pumping not another drop of blood.

With a look of sheer madness on his face, the dwarf poked at the control panel on his wheelchair and came charging at Stone, his face ablaze with fire, his Cheshire cat mouth oozing a foam of rage.

"Bastard, bastard," the thing screamed over and over, at a rare loss for words. Evidently, he had held a certain fondness in his sick heart for Queenie. How many men had they carved up alongside one another? Stone wondered. But as the chair drew closer, he instinctively moved to the side—barely in time, for a stream of slugs poured out of both handles of the dwarf's mobile home and into the wall behind him. Stone reached forward and picked the wretched excuse for a man up by the collar so that it wriggled and struggled in his hand like some hideous creature from the depths of the sea.

"What is the sound of a dwarf smashing into a wall?" Stone asked it, holding the thing up before his eyes. Then pulling back with all his might, he flung the stump creature forward. Poet flew across the room like a fleshy meteor and then slammed into the far wall, where he slid down to the floor and lay in a motionless pile like some sort of holocaust Humpty Dumpty who had fallen off one wall too many, blood oozing out of the pasty flesh.

"I'll get you, Stone," the thing somehow managed to whisper through its smile of pain. "I'll find you, I swear. Wherever you go, I'll, I'll—" Then the small head fell to one shoulder.

Stone lashed his knife hand out at several of them as he

reached for his pistols, which were still holstered and hanging on a rack by the door. But they didn't seem too enthusiastic about actually getting to him, especially after seeing Queenie buy it. Stone threw the gun belts over his shoulder and then grabbed a chair that sat just inside the door. Before they could rush him, he stepped outside and slammed it shut again, wedging the chair frame between the knob and the concrete sidewalk outside. It would hold them long enough for him to get the hell out of this postnuke Sodom and Gomorrah.

CHAPTER
TWENTY

They had brought him back to Denver, to a deserted warehouse in the center of the red light district, which the Slits ran. Stone walked quickly but carefully, checking every doorway, his hand resting on his Uzi, ready to spray out a thirty-round clip at the slightest motions. He reached the front street, where just a few bums and slime wandered around in circles looking for God to drop them a drink. His bike was gone—the other Guardians could be looking for him. He could trust none of them now. It was over. It was time to take this whole town into hell. He slid among the shadows and made his way through the back streets to the Western Tower. He peered from behind garbage cans on a corner two blocks away—but it was bad. If anything, the machine-gun emplacements had been strengthened, and about twenty bikers sat on their humming machines out front, ready to strike.

They were after him. He had just become public enemy

number one to every bastard who wore a skull and mushroom cloud on his back. And he was outnumbered by about two thousand to one. Then he'd just have to take them out before they could take him out. He made his way through the dim streets as the sun tumbled from the far sky as if something had shot it. Whenever he heard the whine of a motor, he dove behind the nearest wrecked car or mound of garbage. Somehow he managed to avoid detection all the way to the edge of the city, where he scrambled up the side of a hill and into some bushes. He stopped to make sure he wasn't being pursued, but not a soul was following behind. Just an empty street in which a few drunks had already passed out before the night had even gotten going.

It took Stone two hours to reach the general location of his hidden Harley 1200 and then another hour just to find the right bunch of ripping thornbushes that camouflaged it. But at last he sat atop the Electroglide on the mountain road overlooking Denver. From a thousand feet up he could see the lights burning throughout the city. It all looked so festive and comforting—a refuge from the cold night. What a laugh. He would take the shadows of the darkest Rocky Mountain night over the monsters that roamed inside human skins down there.

He took out two silencers from the weapons accessories case on the back of the bike and screwed them onto the .44 Redhawk and the Uzi autopistol. The devices added bulk to each pistol, but the element of surprise, the ability to fire without the enemy even knowing where it was coming from made them indispensable tools in the trade of destruction. He loaded the sawed-off 12-gauge and slid it into the fiberglass case built just under the seat on the right side, and then put

a fresh double magazine in the armored box on the back of the front fender that fed to the .50-cal machine gun, three inches of dark steel snout ready to deal death wholesale.

He was ready, except for the final touch. Stone reached around in the wide, cushioned seat and grabbed a long crate from the equipment rack on the back, setting it down just behind him. He pulled open the top. Plastique—packets of it about the size of a softball, with radio-controlled detonator sunk deep inside. It was urban-renewal time—Ranger style.

He roared down the mountain road, opening the bike up to sixty, seventy on a few straightaways, just to get her motor warmed up. She couldn't stall tonight, couldn't falter for a second. But the bull of a machine purred along with a contented growl, as if ready for the hunt, as if in hibernation too long. He reached the plateau on which the city stood and circled all the way around to the north. They might be still looking for him around the southern and eastern portions of Denver—though even that was doubtful. Their ability to be thorough and follow through a coherent plan of operation was not one of their strong points and he would use this to its fullest advantage.

He reached the edge of the city, a portion used only by the poorest of the poor, and made his way slowly down the streets. The funnel of light poured out by his headlamp illuminated countless bodies, some living, some not, that lay around the streets and the sidewalks. Rats scampered off as the bike approached, different parts of human anatomy in their mouths. Stone had to be careful not to ride right over anyone who still breathed. This must be where the Guardians discarded their slaves, whores, passersby that they were through with. It was an open-air graveyard on the other side

of their own city. Even animals treated their dead better than that, Stone thought, with a fury rising in his guts like a Mount St. Helens of emotion. He couldn't help these poor bastards now—any of them. But he could see that they had a fitting memorial—a memorial of fire—to purify their corrupted bodies and cleanse the virus that had infected them.

He slid into the center of Denver at a slow, even speed, his eyes darting around like a bird of prey. It was late—nearly four in the morning. Even the moon had departed long ago from the star-studded heavens, heading for her basement home. Not a man walked the streets to see the solitary leather-jacketed figure riding through the darkness, heaving out little white balls of death that slapped onto girders, windows, porches, and stuck to them like glue. Stone selected as targets all the places he knew were Guardian bars or headquarters. And wherever there were groups of bikes parked along the street, he dropped a present right into the middle of them. He sped through the streets of the city for nearly an hour, depositing the little eggs everywhere. With the radio detonators inside the plastique tuned to four different frequencies, he set the city up into quadrants, putting all the explosives in each sector on one frequency so he could blow them in a coordinated way.

"Stage one complete," he said to himself through chattering teeth as he looked down at the almost empty box on the seat behind him. His face felt as if a polar bear had been teething on it; it was red and half frostbitten from riding around in the freezing temperatures. He knew his body temperature was way down, perhaps dangerously low, but he was almost ready to light the cake—and that would warm things up considerably.

Stone had seen an oil truck pull up the night before under heavy guard. Gasoline was as precious as ammunition in the year 1995, and the Guardians kept their supplies under lock and key in a barbed-wire fenced area where three of the long, cylindrical tankers now stood parked. Stone drove his bike to within two blocks of the Guardian headquarters in the state capitol and hid it in an alley behind some rusting garbage cans. He made his way like a cat, prowling through the dark, deserted streets, his silenced Uzi gripped firmly in his right hand, his eyes wide with the excitement of imminent battle.

Within fifteen minutes he was staring through the steel mesh of the fence at the three wide gas trucks sitting side by side like so many fatted pigs waiting for the slaughter. Five Guardians in various states of consciousness, from barely awake to comatose, sat around a fire, sleeping bags covering their big frames like cocoons. There was no way he could climb the fence with its ribbons of razor wire running along the top, so Stone moved on his toes around the side until he came to a padlocked door. He aimed the silencer-extended automatic pistol dead center of the lock, set it to semiauto, and pulled the trigger twice. The pistol jerked slightly in his hand and spat out the 9mm slugs with two whooshes of air. The lock made a sharp but not very loud sound as the bullets pinged off of it and then cracked right down the middle, bending over on itself.

Stone ripped the broken lock free and tore through the door toward the closest of the big diesel tankers. But he had barely gone two yards when a figure came from out of the darkness, holding a rifle at his chest. Stone dove just as the biker sighted him and in midair ripped off a hail of slugs, emptying half the magazine into the man's body. The slugs

tore down the flesh, starting at the throat and ending at the groin, cutting him like a pair of scissors into bloody paper dolls.

But the dead man's fingers somehow pulled his Winchester .30–30 as he fell to the earth. Stone ripped the clip from the bottom of the Uzi and threw it away instantly, replacing it with another from the utility belt around his waist. He tore around the front of the near tanker and came face to face with the other four Guardians already on their feet, assorted guns in their hands. But his finger was already on the trigger, spraying a line of fire at waist level in a fifteen-foot radius in front of him. Four guns fired, but their shooters were already falling sideways, eyes hazing over, unfocused and dumb, as spouts of blood poured from the red holes that dotted their bodies. Their shots flew wildly into the air, missing Stone by yards.

He caught hold of the freezing steel door frame and pulled himself up into the driver's seat, searching frantically for the keys in the darkness. At last he located them behind the sun visor and with trembling, half-numb fingers jammed them into the ignition. He turned them, and the fifty-foot super diesel tanker roared to life, her chromium cabin vibrating like a malted-milk shaker. The dashboard of the thing looked like it belonged in a spaceship, but Stone didn't have time to worry about it as the gunshots had woken another group of bikers in a nearby building. They ran from the doorway, pants only half on, and rushed toward him.

"Well, here goes," Stone said to himself and the truck, patting it on one of its brightly lit display panels. "I hope you're user friendly." He slammed the steel dragon into gear and then pushed his foot to the floor. The tanker responded

without a moment's hesitation as it roared forward and right through the cable fence, snapping it in two like a piece of string, sending pieces of it flying off. He ripped the long stick shift into second gear and felt the vehicle respond, gaining speed by the second. The bikers leaped out of the way as the whale-sized truck came barreling down on them, two of them not quite making it. They disappeared beneath the wheels as if swallowed whole and emerged as little more than red mud sprayed out from the huge back wheels.

He wheeled the thirty-ton vehicle, filled to the very rafters with high-octane gasoline, through the streets as if he were driving a stock car at the races. He'd have to move fast—they already knew something was up. Lights were snapping on in windows, bikes revving up. Within a minute he had picked up something of a posse of wild-eyed bikers firing everything they had at the truck as they had obviously decided to blow the whole damned thing up rather than let some bastard get away with it. And with the superior speed of the bikes, Stone saw two of them looming into view in this side mirror. Keeping his right hand on the wheel, he ripped out the .44 cannon and aimed it out the opened window on his left. A biker shot into view, his head bobbing as he searched for the driver inside. Suddenly he caught sight of Stone looking down at him—and then was blasted by fire from the muzzle that was pointing at him. His face disappeared into something red as the bike veered sharply off the street and slammed right through a shop window, slashing what remained of the corpse atop it with a thousand shards of glass.

But they kept coming—in the side mirror he could see them gaining every second. Stone searched frantically around the ultramodern dashboard filled with levers and dials and

windows giving digital readouts of every aspect of the super diesel's systems. He saw a button marked "AUTO PUMP" and slammed his hand down on it. A valve opened automatically on the back of the truck and released a river of high-test gasoline onto the central thoroughfare of Denver. He watched through the rear-view as he saw the avenue begin to shimmer with the liquid for at least a block and then slammed the button again. The valve whirred closed and the flow stopped.

The first few bikers who reached the inch-deep lake of gasoline roared right into it, pulling their feet up out of the way. The fifth and sixth motorcycles also rolled through it in pursuit. But the seventh bike skidded suddenly halfway through and flipped over on its side. The sparks of metal hitting concrete at fifty miles an hour instantly ignited the entire block and all forty-three bikers on it into a sheet of fire that reached six stories high and filled half the city with the reflection of its flames.

Stone slowed down slightly at the main intersection and wheeled the huge tanker around a corner so that its entire weight shifted and the whole right side of the vehicle lifted a foot off the ground, slamming back down again like a dinosaur as he straightened the wheel out. Even from twenty blocks off he could see it—far down the avenue was the capitol, its gold dome glistening in the predawn sky like a jeweled spire from some supernatural realm. Rommel and the dwarf and all the other misfits, perverts, and monstrosities who ran the town would be in there, wondering what the hell was going on. They would be rising now from their bleeding teenaged whores. Well, this was just to say good-bye—and to thank them for the delightful visit. A personal message when nothing else would do.

He waited until he was five blocks away and then tied the wheel down and lashed the accelerator to the floor with some nylon cord he had brought. He slapped two proximity-detonated plastique packs on the dashboard and then opened the door of the speeding truck and jumped off. He hit the hard street in a roll, spinning over a dozen times before he came to a stop, but the thick leather of the Guardian gang jacket he wore protected him from everything but the pain. He rose to his feet and saw the long steel cigar tearing ass straight down the street. It hit the sidewalk and rolled right up on it, smashing through the small guardpost in which two bikers slept never even knowing what it was that turned them into paste. The gas truck shot across the marbled stone terrace and then up the thirty or so hand-carved stairs that led to the Guardian headquarters. It seemed to accelerate as it flew, as if getting into the kamikaze mission with its own vehicular dreams of glory. Forty tons of steel and gasoline smashed through the oak doors of the Colorado capitol, taking with it the walls, the windows, the whole front of the monumental building. The truck charged into the carpeted foyer, where a dozen or so bikers lay curled up in unconscious balls on the floor.

Then the plastique went off. For some reason it took a few seconds for the liquid cargo to ignite—just enough time for those present to open their eyes and see a gasoline truck with its front end on fire at their feet. But only for a second. Then the gas caught.

From where he stood, now four blocks off as he ran back to his bike hidden nearby, Stone felt the shock wave of the explosion lift him right off his feet and carry him several yards before throwing him down on his side. Then the noise

followed—so deafening that he instinctively threw his hands over his ears as he spun around to see what he had wrought. The building was exploding out in every direction, walls, windows, thousands of fragments shooting out in a great wave of smoke and plaster. The entire golden dome of the capitol was rising into the air from the tremendous pressure generated by the instantaneous explosion of twenty thousand gallons of high-test. But even as the great structure rose with impossible, slow grace into the night air, it seemed to be a hallucination, an illusion, and as he watched, it disintegrated before his eyes into a golden rain which covered everything it touched with the shimmering dust of a dream.

Stone rose to his feet and remounted the cycle as the initial blast settled back down in a blizzard of particles and the entire circular structure burst into a pillar of flame. He shot the other way, toward the Western Tower—and he prayed, after all this, that April would be there. His hope was that the explosion at the capitol would draw some of those protecting the tower away. And when he arrived he could see it had worked—up to a point. A number of them had ridden off, but there was still three full teams manning the front emplacements. Stone stopped the bike a block away and got off it. He could see them looking at him nervously, clicking back their releases on the big tripod-mounted automatic rifles and machine guns. He walked to the left side of the bike and undid the catch of the Luchaire mini-rocket launcher, pulling the system out and around so it was aimed toward the front door of the building, roughly toward the central machine-gun nest. But from what he remembered, pinpoint accuracy was not of the essence with the 89mm rocket.

Stone could see several of the Guardians standing up on

the sandbagged positions and looking at him with binoculars. He waved and pulled the trigger of the ten-inch-thick launch tube. The entire bike shuddered for a moment from the recoil as the projectile streaked down the street just feet above the ground, leaving a white trail behind it. The Guardians who saw it coming didn't have time to scream. The sixteen-inch-long missile slammed into the front emplacement, sending it up in a hurricane of blood and gristle, throwing sandbags flying like children's blocks. Every Guardian within fifteen feet was torn to shreds by the shrapnel-projecting warhead as thousands of red-hot spinning pieces of steel buzz-sawed their way into stomachs and brain cavities.

Stone jumped up on the bike and shot forward through the smoke. He pulled up with all his body weight as he reached the tumbled, blood-drenched sandbags and the bike lifted into the air, shooting up over them as if up a ramp. He soared a good six feet in the air over the bodies and the twisted machine guns and came down hard just inside the front entrance door. The bike skidded sideways into the lobby, and Stone did nearly a complete three-sixty, anchoring one foot on the floor and letting the bike spin around him. He pulled the trigger of the front-mounted .50 as he saw motion from behind what had once been an information booth. The wooden desk exploded into toothpicks, and two more Guardians, shotguns in their hands, came flying out, sawed into bloody, asymmetrical pieces.

Stone looked around and saw no one else, not anyone who was capable of moving anyway, and wheeled the big bike behind a reception desk, turning it toward the front door so he could beat a hasty retreat. The elevators weren't working, so Stone took the fire stairs, flying up them two at a time.

On the tenth floor the door was locked, but a shot from the mag exploded the entire lock and doorknob from the frame. He kicked it and came in flying. There was no one there. The place was empty. He knew his information was right. It had to be the tenth floor. Stone stormed down the darkened hallway, kicking doors open with every step. Disheveled mattresses, torn clothes were inside—but no girls. In the last room he heard a noise in the closet and aimed the Redhawk.

"Step out or die. Immediately," he yelled, in no mood to play any games. The door tentatively opened, and a very wide and very short woman stepped out with a garish red wig and a solid inch of pancake makeup on her heavily lined face.

"Who the hell are you?" Stone asked, letting the weapon fall a little as he saw that she couldn't be of any danger—not with a face so contorted with fear. "Relax, relax," he said a little more softly, realizing she was so scared she couldn't speak.

"Now, who are you?" he went on as the huge-bosomed female caught her breath.

"I'm Madam Xavier. I—I run this place—did run it. Took care of the girls, got 'em nice and clean and pretty for the winners of the games."

"But where are they?" Stone went on in desperation. "They were supposed to be here."

"They was here till about three hours ago, then the men came to claim their prizes. It was a madhouse in here—they was fighting each other over who got which one, but finally—"

"Listen," Stone said, taking her by the shoulders gently but firmly. "Was there a blonde girl about fifteen among them?

Her name was April." The woman looked down, unable to meet his eyes, fearful that the wrong answer would mean her death. "Tell me, tell me," Stone demanded. "Tell me the truth. I swear to you, whatever it is I'll let you live. You walk out now. The truth."

"She was here, mister," the woman said softly, tears beginning to fall down her powdered face. "She was, but they took her and you ain't never going to see her again."

CHAPTER TWENTY-ONE

"You said you wouldn't kill me," the whorekeeper cried out as she saw the fury build up in Stone's face like a lightning bolt with no place to discharge.

"Get out of here," he said disgustedly, pointing with the 9mm autopistol toward the door. "Wait," he yelled just as she started to step through. "Where did he take her? Who was he?"

"It—it was the one they call Straight Razor because he carries 'em all over his body in little holsters. He's a mean one, he is, mister. He took her down to Pueblo where he's the leader of the gang there. If you're after him," she whispered, "take my advice—get yourself a new girl, they're cheap enough—and go home." With that she turned and ran down the stairs as fast as her chubby, short legs could move.

Stone looked around for a moment in a daze and then spotted something shiny on one side of the ripped mattress.

He reached down and picked it up, and his eyes misted up the instant he touched it. It was April's charm bracelet, filled with miniature dogs, guitars, tennis rackets, and more things than he had ever been able to stop and count. He stood up, putting it deep in an inner pocket. Whatever had happened to her, she was still alive. And she would want it again. Want it desperately, for it might well be the last beautiful thing she would possess in this world.

He tore back down the stairs and out into the street, past the bodies with bubbling pits for stomachs and dirt for eyes, and found his bike. There was just one thing left for him to do before he set out after her. Something that had been on his mind since the first moment he had set foot in this hellhole of a town. He pulled the accelerator to the max and tore down Fairfax Avenue toward whore row and Rommel's bar. Bikers were streaming up and down the streets in a killing mood—only they didn't know who it was they were supposed to kill. Stone was just another black-jacketed biker hunched over his machine.

The fire from the devastated capitol building was still burning brightly twenty blocks behind, lighting up the gathering clouds above with groping orange fingers. It was time to light a few more. Stone reached for the radio transmitter controlling detonation commands to the little Easter eggs he had laid out. He set the dial to one of the four frequencies and pressed the "fire" button. To his right the entire sky seemed to turn into a single ball of white as the high explosives went up in a microsecond, blasting everything around them into burning sawdust. He changed the frequency and pressed "fire" again. This time the western sky was suddenly filled with a mountain of spinning, fiery debris which flew

like an entire garbage dump on fire into the sky. He quickly set the other two wavelengths and set off another two quadrants' worth of death. Numerous secondaries could be heard everywhere as gas tanks and munitions storage dumps went up in blasts that seemed to shake the very granite foundations of the city.

The Guardians were in sheer panic, riding madly in every direction like cockroaches scampering from their burning nest. Flames literally encircled the city, now spreading quickly as brisk arctic winds began ripping in over the mountains. Stone tore down the main strip that Rommel's bar was on and pulled to a sharp stop in front. He stepped off the bike, setting it on its kickstand, and started toward the door.

"Hold it, Stone," a voice yelled from behind him before he had gone a step. "Don't turn around and don't move fast. You got six guns trained on you right now—and every one of them would like nothing more than to blast your fucking face into mush that a maggot wouldn't touch." Stone froze in his tracks. It was Rommel. It was impossible, but the man was still alive. Moving as slowly as a lengthening shadow, Stone shifted his weight toward the bike, keeping his hands high.

"I had a hunch you were going to pay a little visit here," Rommel growled through his tangled beard. "In fact, I had a hunch you were going to visit the dome too—though I didn't realize you were going to come so well prepared. I had my eye on you from the start, Stone. I never trusted you for a second. Could have killed you at any time, but I wanted to find out your game. What is your game, Stone? 'Cause it's dying time no matter how you look at it. But if you tell

me I'll just kill you. If you don't, I'll do things to you that would give the devil bad dreams."

Stone worked his way over so his leg was touching the bike. Looking forward and down, he could see them in the rear-view mirror standing directly behind him in the shadows of the fires burning on all four sides of the city—Rommel in the center with a 12-gauge pump in his hands, and on each side of him Eddie and Slash, Cruiser and Three Toes—all of Stone's favorite people in one place at one time, and all aiming some piece of firepower or other at his back that would turn his spinal cord into something resembling a broken umbrella within seconds.

Stone always liked it when he had nothing to lose. Once again it made things so simple. "My game is—" he shouted, to divert their attention from their trigger fingers to their ears. Which it did—giving him the fraction of a second he needed to click the firing lever of the Luchaire, which was locked in place on the bike, aiming straight backward. The second he pulled it, Stone dove forward as two or three shots rang out, pinging off his bike. Then there was a roar that shook the very lining of his skull as the antitank missile shot forward, covering the distance between it and its target in a tenth of a second and slammed into Rommel's chest. The missile, triggered for impact, disintegrated the biker top man as if he had never existed, leaving just a fine red spray that spread up and down the street along with the shock waves of the blast. The other Guardians were blown to bits, all of them within direct range of the blast. Arms, heads, and blood-coated, unrecognizable things flew off into the street and into the windows of Rommel's bar, cracking them and frosting them over with a pink coating.

Stone rose, his head still filled with the booming decibelage of the explosion. He could hardly hear, although nobody was talking. He walked forward, slowly taking out the 9mm as he looked among the pieces of sizzling flesh. But there was no need. None of these would ever hurt him, or anyone again. He walked into Rommel's bar and stood at one end, looking down at the rows of animals and reptiles he had seen imprisoned behind Plexiglas. Somehow it seemed to be a perfect metaphor for the whole damned place—a prison in which living things went slowly mad. He walked over to a wall and took down a huge fire ax with a fifteen-pound head painted bright red. It would do.

He walked up to the closest enclosure and looked down. The rattlers inside stirred, sensing something, and gathered in the corner farthest from the human who kept looking at them. Stone knew it was mad, totally insane. If there were lunatic asylums around anymore, they would doubtless lock him up and throw away the key. But there *were* no madhouses—the patients were running the show now. He might as well join them.

He brought the ax blade down on the padlock at the bottom, and the casing burst apart as if a cannon shell had hit it. Stone lifted the side of the enclosure so that it opened out, depositing the squirming snakes on the floor. He pulled away, but somehow they knew he had helped them and, besides, they weren't sticking around so someone could imprison them again. They moved along the floor and out the door in a flash, heading toward the nearest woods they could find. Next was a pair of raccoons who jumped around their glass case in panic and excitement, blinking their ringed eyes at him. Again

the ax lifted and descended and two more creatures shot out the door without even looking back.

It took him fifteen minutes, but Stone freed every damned thing in the place, whether it wanted to be freed or not— lizards, gìla monsters, scorpions, coyotes, foxes, two mountain lions, a small black bear, and numerous other scaled and furred animals of the wild who had been unfortunate enough to have fallen into the hands of human beings, the cruelest species on earth.

He came to the very last of the cases and looked inside. An English pit bull, a fighting dog, this one of tremendous size, stared up at him with steady, unfearful eyes. The dog was beautiful, and its eyes looked almost like those of a wise man—liquid pools which absorbed Stone's glance without a ripple.

"Stand back, pooch," Stone yelled as he slammed the ax down with all his might. The lock shattered, and the dog pushed with its head and opened the confining Plexiglas by itself.

"Good boy. Smart, aren't you?" Stone said with a smile, scratching the seventy pounds of pure muscle on the head. He had read that this was a dangerous breed, originally created to hunt tigers, and that their jaws could crush bone into powder. But this one looked friendly enough, wagging its tail, licking his hand affectionately. It knew instinctively who was friend and who was enemy. "Well, gotta go, fella," Stone said, slapping it on the side. "You get out of here. Find yourself a nice master. Come on now—go." He clapped his hands briskly and made a waving motion, but the animal only thought he wanted to play and jumped around in front of him. He felt bad for it. But it would survive. The dog was

strong like steel beneath his hands. It would live. It would have to.

Stone planted his last two packets of explosive and headed outside, walking past the bodies that still steamed as if not quite well-done enough. The dog sniffed at them, growled, and then stepped back, not wanting to sully its paws with their foul remains. Stone mounted the bike and eased it forward down the street as a light snow began falling so that the wheels carved out ridged trails in the white frosting. But he had only gone a few blocks when he heard heavy breathing and looked around to see the English bull running alongside him just behind the bike. Stone came to a stop and stared down at the thing.

"Get out of here!" he yelled. "There's no room for a dog! You'll have to find a new home somewhere." He spread his arms apart, as if indicating the streets around them might be a good place to start. But with the flames rising and the smoke filling the skies, he thought better of the idea and lowered them. "Oh, fuck it," he shouted and turned the throttle, spinning off and away, leaving the animal tripping on its own paws in the snow.

He rode to the southern edge of town and then up the side of the mountain that stood before him. When he was at about a thousand feet elevation, Stone stopped the bike and eased it in over at the side of the road. He sat on the big Harley, its engine hot from the hours of riding, and looked down over Denver. It was aflame in a hundred places, spirals of fire eddying up into the air, their smoke joining in a single great cloud far overhead that blanketed the area for miles. Stone had planted the bombs where they would do the most damage to the Guardians. He had tried to

protect the regular citizens—what there were of them. But as in any war, they would be hurt as well—innocent people killed, homes burned. But it had to be. To root out the cancer, nearby cells were sometimes destroyed. The virus that had infected their city had been badly weakened by Stone. It was up to the citizens of the city to decide what they would do with the patient.

He breathed out a deep sigh as if exhaling all the death and blood he had witnessed, and caused, tonight. He would find her, find April if he had to follow her into the lion's den. He wouldn't rest until she was safe again—and until whoever harmed her was lying in the cold earth.

The sound of a branch cracking made him reach for his Uzi, swinging it up and around set on full auto. But his face broke into a broad smile as he saw that it was just the dog, huffing and puffing up the road behind him. It came right up alongside him, blowing a stream of fog up into his face.

"You don't give up, do you, dog?" Stone laughed, looking down at the handsome creature with its shining white coat and rows of daggerlike teeth. The dog jumped on the bike behind him as if it had ridden that way before and nestled down all snug and comfortable. Stone turned around, looking at the white cannonball with disbelief.

"Listen, pal, you don't understand," Stone said, trying to sternly lecture the dog into realizing what was in his best interest. "Where I'm going, I don't think I'm coming out. I wouldn't have time to stop and feed you, plus I'll most likely be dead in a few days. I'd be a bad master. All these things are too much for a dog to have to worry about."

He looked deep into the animal's eyes, which glistened back at him with simple good humor. It barked, licked its nose with a long red tongue, and then barked again as if telling him to get on with the journey.

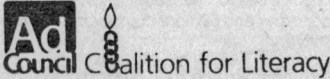